⬨ W9-AER-700

"I continue to think that she is the most competent of contemporary Canadian writers—clear-eyed, keen-eyed, unpretentious, honest."

—*Montreal Star*

"I cannot recall ever reading a collection of short stories which does what A BIRD IN THE HOUSE does with admirable and surprising simplicity."

—*The Fiddlehead*

"In a style that is totally authentic, free of artifice and of any straining for effect . . . Mrs. Laurence has portrayed it all superbly with her remarkable facility for making uncommonly good stories out of commonplace events."

—*Toronto Globe and Mail*

"A child growing up on the Prairies during the Depression . . . When Mrs. Laurence approaches this oft-told tale she breathes fresh life into it; she rescues it from the quicksand of banality and makes it, each time, a fresh work of art."

—*The Vancouver Sun*

Gramley Library
Salem College
Winston-Salem, NC 27108

Bantam-Seal Books by Margaret Laurence
Ask your bookseller for the books you have missed

A BIRD IN THE HOUSE
THE DIVINERS
THE FIRE DWELLERS
HEART OF A STRANGER
JASON'S QUEST
A JEST OF GOD
THE STONE ANGEL

A Bird
in the House

Margaret Laurence

Seal Books
are published by
McClelland and Stewart-Bantam Limited
Toronto

Gramley Library
Salem College
Winston-Salem, NC 27108

*This low-priced Bantam Book
has been completely reset in a type face
designed for easy reading, and was printed
from new plates. It contains the complete
text of the original hard-cover edition.*
NOT ONE WORD HAS BEEN OMITTED.

A BIRD IN THE HOUSE

*A Seal Book / published by arrangement with
McClelland and Stewart Limited*

PRINTING HISTORY

*McClelland and Stewart edition published February 1970
2nd printing . . . . November 1972*

*Seal edition / October 1978
2nd printing . . . . . February 1980
3rd printing . . . . April 1981
4th printing . . . . September 1981*

*These stories have been published or broadcast by the fol-
lowing:*
"The Sound of the Singing"—*Winter's Tales 9;*
"To Set Our House in Order"—*Ladies Home Journal, Argosy,
Modern Canadian Stories;*
"Mask of the Bear"—*Chatelaine, Winter's Tales 11;*
"The Loons"—Canadian Broadcasting Corporation, *Atlantic
Advocate;*
"A Bird in the House"—*Atlantic Monthly, Winter's Tales from
Canada;*
"Horse of the Night"—*Chatelaine, Winter's Tales 15;*
"The Half Husky" (first published as "Nanuk")—Canadian
Broadcasting Corporation, *Argosy.*

*All rights reserved.
Copyright © 1963, 1964, 1965, 1966,
1967, 1970, 1974 by Margaret Laurence.
This book may not be reproduced in whole or in part, by
mimeograph or any other means, without permission.
For information address: McClelland and Stewart Limited,
25 Hollinger Road, Toronto, Ontario M4B 3G2.*

ISBN 0-7704-1742-6

*Seal Books are published by McClelland and Stewart-Bantam
Limited. Its trademark, consisting of the words "Seal Books"
and the portrayal of a seal, is the property of McClelland and
Stewart-Bantam Limited, 25 Hollinger Road, Toronto, Ontario
M4B 3G2. This trademark has been duly registered in the Trade-
marks Office of Canada. The trademark, consisting of the word
"Bantam" and the portrayal of a rooster, is the property of and
is used with the consent of Bantam Books, Inc., 666 Fifth Ave-
nue, New York, New York 10103. The trademark has been duly
registered in the Trademark Office of Canada and elsewhere.*

PRINTED IN THE UNITED STATES OF AMERICA

13 12 11 10 9 8 7 6 5

FOR

my aunts and my children

CONTENTS

A BIRD IN THE HOUSE

The Sound
of the Singing

That house in Manawaka is the one which, more than
any other, I carry with me. Known to the rest of the
town as "the old Connor place" and to the family
as the Brick House, it was plain as the winter turnips
in its root cellar, sparsely windowed as some crusad-
er's embattled fortress in a heathen wilderness, its
rooms in a perpetual gloom except in the brief height
of summer. Many other brick structures had existed in
Manawaka for as much as half a century, but at the
time when my grandfather built his house, part dwelling place and part massive monument, it had been the
first of its kind.

Set back at a decent distance from the street,
it was screened by a line of spruce trees whose green-
black branches swept down to the earth like the
sternly protective wings of giant hawks. Spruce was
not indigenous to that part of the prairies. Timothy
Connor had brought the seedlings all the way from
Galloping Mountain, a hundred miles north, not on
whim, one may be sure, but feeling that they were the
trees for him. By the mid-thirties, the spruces were
taller than the house, and two generations of children
had clutched at boughs which were as rough and
hornily knuckled as the hands of old farmers, and had
swung themselves up to secret sanctuaries. On the
lawn a few wild blue violets dared to grow, despite
frequent beheadings from the clanking guillotine lawn
mower, and mauve-flowered Creeping Charley insin-
uated deceptively weak-looking tendrils up to the

very edges of the flower beds where helmeted snapdragon stood in precision.

We always went for Sunday dinner to the Brick House, the home of my mother's parents. This particular day my father had been called out to South Wachakwa, where someone had pneumonia, so only my mother and myself were flying down the sidewalk, hurrying to get there. My mother walked with short urgent steps, and I had to run to keep up, which I did not like having to do, for I was ten that spring and needed my dignity.

"Dad said you shouldn't walk so fast because of the baby. I heard him."

My father was a doctor, and like many doctors, his advice to his own family was of an exceedingly casual nature. My mother's prenatal care, apart from "For Pete's sake, honey, quit running around like a chicken with its head cut off," consisted mainly of admonitions to breathe deeply and drink plenty of water.

"Mercy," my mother replied, "I don't have to slow up that much, I should hope. Get a move on, Vanessa. It's nearly five, and we should've been there by now. I suppose Edna will have the dinner all ready, and there won't be a thing for me to do. I wish to heaven she wouldn't, but try to tell her. Anyway, you know how your grandfather hates people to be late."

When we got to the Brick House, my mother stopped hurrying, knowing that Grandfather would be watching from the bay window. She tidied my hair, which was fine and straight and tended to get in my eyes, and she smoothed down the collar of the white middy which I hated and resented having to wear today with my navy pleated skirt as though it had still been winter.

"Your summer dresses are all up to your neck," my mother had said, "and we just can't manage a new one this year, but I'm certainly not going to have you going down there looking like a hooligan."

Now that the pace of our walking had slowed,

I began to hop along the sidewalk trying to touch the crooked lines where the cement had been frost-heaved, some winter or other, and never repaired. The ants made their homes there, and on each fissure a neat mound of earth appeared. I carefully tamped one down with my foot, until the ant castle was flattened to nothing. Then I hopped on, chanting.

"Step on a crack, break your grandfather's back."

"That's not very nice, Vanessa," my mother said. "Anyway, I always thought it was your mother's back."

"Well?" I said accusingly, hurt that she could imagine the substitution to have been accidental, for I had genuinely thought it would please her.

"Try not to tear up and down stairs like you did last week," my mother said anxiously. "You're too old for that kind of shenanigans."

Grandfather was standing on the front porch to greet us. He was a tall husky man, drum-chested, and once he had possessed great muscular strength. That simple power was gone now, but age had not stooped him.

"Well, Beth, you're here," Grandfather said. "Past five, ain't it?"

"It's only ten to," my mother said defensively. "I hoped Ewen might be back—that's why I waited. He had to go out to South Wachakwa on a call."

"You'd think a man could stay home on a Sunday," Grandfather said.

"Good grief, Father," my mother said, "people get sick on Sundays the same as any other day."

But she said it under her breath, so he did not hear her.

"Well, come in, come in," he said. "No use standing around here all day. Go and say hello to your grandmother, Vanessa."

Ample and waistless in her brown silk dress, Grandmother was sitting in the dining room watching the canary. The bird had no name. She did not believe in bestowing names upon non-humans, for a name to her meant a christening, possible only for Christians.

She called the canary "Birdie," and maintained that this was not like a real name. It was swaying lightly on the bird-swing in its cage, its attentive eyes fixed upon her. She often sat here, quietly and apparently at ease, not feeling it necessary to be talking or doing, beside the window sill with its row of African violets in old ginger jars that had been painted orange. She would try to coax the canary into its crystal trilling, but it was a surly creature and obliged only occasionally. She liked me to sit here with her, and sometimes I did, but I soon grew impatient and began squirming, until Grandmother would smile and say, "All right, pet, you run along, now," and then I would be off like buckshot. When I asked my grandmother if the bird minded being there, she shook her head and said no, it had been there always and wouldn't know what to do with itself outside, and I thought this must surely be so, for it was a family saying that she couldn't tell a lie if her life depended on it.

"Hello, pet," Grandmother said. "Did you go to Sunday school?"

"Yes."

"What did you learn?" Grandmother asked, not prying or demanding, but confidently, serenely.

I was prepared, for the question was the same each week. I rarely listened in Sunday school, finding it more entertaining to compose in my head stories of spectacular heroism in which I figured as central character, so I never knew what the text had been. But I had read large portions of the Bible by myself, for I was constantly hard-up for reading material, so I had no trouble in providing myself with a verse each week before setting out for the Brick House. My lines were generally of a warlike nature, for I did not favour the meek stories and I had no use at all for the begats.

"*How are the mighty fallen in the midst of the battle,*" I replied instantly.

"Second Samuel," Grandmother said, nodding her head. "That's very nice, dear."

4

I was not astonished that my grandmother thought the bloody death of Jonathan was very nice, for this was her unvarying response, whatever the verse. And in fact it was not strange, for to her everything in the Bible was as gentle as she herself. The swords were spiritual only, strokes of lightness and dark, and the wounds poured cochineal.

Grandfather tramped into the dining room. His hair was yellowish white, but once it had been as black as my own, and his brown beaked leathery face was still handsome.

"You'd best come into the living room, Agnes," he said. "No use waiting here. Beth says Ewen's gone away out to South Wachakwa. It'll be a wonder if we get our dinner at all tonight."

Grandmother rose. "Yes, I was just coming in."

Grandfather walked over to the window and peered at the plants on the sill.

"Them jars could do with a coat of paint," he said. "I've got some enamel left in the basement. It's that bottle-green I used on the tool-shed."

"Is there no orange left?" Grandmother enquired.

"No. It's all used up. What's the matter with bottle-green?"

"Oh, nothing's the matter with it, I guess. I just wondered, that's all."

"I'll do them first thing tomorrow, then," Grandfather said decisively.

No tasks could be undertaken today, but there was no rule against making plans for Monday, so my grandfather invariably spent the Sabbath in this manner. Thwarted, but making the best of a bad lot, he lumbered around the house like some great wakeful bear waiting for the enforced hibernation of Sunday to be over. He stopped at the hall door now and rattled it, running hard expert fingers along the brass hinges.

"Hinge is loose," he said. "The pin's worn. I'll have to go down to the store and see if they've got one. That Barnes probably won't have the right size—he's

5

got no notion of stock. Maybe I've got an extra one
in the basement. Yes, I have an idea there's one there.
I'll just step down and have a look."

I heard him clumping down the basement steps,
and soon from the area of his work-bench there arose
the soft metallic jangle of nails and bolts, collected
oddments being sifted through. I glanced at my grandmother, but if she was relieved that he was rummag-
ing down there, she gave no sign.

I did not know then the real torment that the day
of rest was for him, so I had no patience with his
impatience. What I did know, however, was that if he
had been any other way he would not have passed
muster in Manawaka. He was widely acknowledged
as an upright man. It would have been a disgrace if he
had been known by the opposite word, which was
"downright." A few of my friends had downright
grandfathers. They were a deep mortification to their
families, these untidy old men who sat on the Bank of
Montreal steps in the summertime and spat amber
tobacco jets onto the dusty sidewalk. They were described as "downright worthless" or "downright lazy,"
the two terms being synonymous. These shadows of
wastrels, these flimsy remnants of past profligates,
with their dry laughter like the cackle of crows or the
crackling of fallen leaves underfoot, embarrassed me
terribly, although I did not have any idea why. Walking down main street, I would avoid looking at them,
feeling somehow that they should not be on view, that
they should be hidden away in an attic along with the
other relics too common to be called antiques and too
broken to be of any further use. Yet I was inexplicably
drawn to them, too.

With Grandfather safely occupied, one danger for
me was temporarily over, for if he could think of
nothing else to do, he would sit me down on a footstool beside his chair and make me listen, fidgeting
with boredom, while he talked of the past. To me
there was nothing at all remarkable in the fact that he

had come out west by sternwheeler and had walked the hundred-odd miles from Winnipeg to Manawaka. Unfortunately, he had not met up with any slit-eyed and treacherous Indians or any mad trappers, but only with ordinary farmers who had given him work shoeing their horses, for he was a blacksmith. He had been the first blacksmith in Manawaka, and finally had saved enough money to set himself up in the hardware business. He frequently related the epic of that significant day.

"I mind well the day I sold out the smithy to Bill Saunders. He was my helper in them days. He died of a growth only last year, and no wonder. He was always a great man for eating fried stuff. I used to tell him it coats the inside of your stomach, but he never paid heed. Well, I'd rented the store space in the old Carmichael block, and I says to Billy, 'I'm going into hardware and if you want the smithy, she's yours for five hundred on the anvil.' He laid down his money, just like that. I picked it up and walked out and I never shod another horse from that day to this. It was hard going in them days, to make the store pay, but I used to load up the buckboard with kettles and axes and that, and take it all around the countryside, and I done a sight better than I would've if I'd sat at home like some fellows I could mention, just waiting for the business to come to me."

I had been trained in both politeness and prudence, so I always said "Gee" in an impressed voice, but it did not seem very exciting to me. I could not imagine the store looking any other way than it did now, a drab place full of kitchen utensils and sawblades and garden tools and kegs of nails. It was not even Connor's Hardware any longer, for Grandfather had sold it a few months ago and had officially retired. He still felt as though he were in the business, however, and would often go down to the store and give good advice to Mr. Barnes, the present owner. Once he took me down with him, and I pretended to be studying the paint charts while Grandfather held forth and Mr. Barnes kept saying, "Well, well, that's a thought all right, yessiree, I'll have to think about that, Mr. Connor." Finally Grandfather went stomping home and said to Grandmother, "The man's a downright fool, and lazy as a pet pig, I'll tell you that much," and my grandmother chirped softly to my aunt, "Edna, make your father a nice cup of tea, will you, pet?"

Aunt Edna and my mother were talking in the kitchen now, so I went out. My mother was the eldest in the family of five, and Aunt Edna was the youngest, and while both had the Connor black hair and blue eyes, they were not alike in appearance. My mother was slight and fine-boned, with long-fingered hands like those on my Chinese princess doll, and feet that Aunt Edna enviously called "aristocratic," which meant narrow. "It's a poor family can't afford one lady," my mother would reply ironically, for we all knew she worked as hard as anyone. Aunt Edna, on the other hand, was handsome and strong but did not like being so. She said she had feet like scows, and she was constantly asking if we thought she had put on weight. My mother, torn between honesty and affection, would reply, "Not so anyone would really notice."

I climbed up on the high kitchen stool, as unobtrusively as possible. I was a professional listener. I had long ago discovered it was folly to try to conceal oneself. The best concealment was to sit quietly in plain view.

"He's always been so active," my mother was saying. "It's understandable, Edna."

"It's all right for you," my aunt said. "Ken Barnes doesn't phone you to complain."

"I know," my mother said.

She leaned against the kitchen cabinet, and all at once I saw the intricate lines of tiredness in her face. Perhaps they had been there all along, but I had never before noticed them. The sight frightened me, for I still needed the conviction that no one except

myself ever suffered anything. Aunt Edna, too, was
scrutinizing her.

"You need a few more smocks, Beth. I thought
I'd run up a couple for you on the machine. I've got
that rose crepe—I never wear it here. The colour
would suit you."

"What? Do sewing, with this house to run? You
haven't the time, Edna. Don't be silly."

My mother disliked rose intensely, but Aunt Edna
had forgotten. The dress had been my aunt's best one,
which she had bought when she went to Winnipeg a
few years before, to take a commercial course.

"I've got nothing to do with my evenings," Aunt
Edna said. "I can't just sit around and twiddle my
thumbs, can I? It's settled, then. I'll get at it next
week."

"Well, thanks," my mother said. "It's very good of
you. What are we going to do about the other, Edna?"

"What can we do? I'm certainly not tackling him
about it, are you?"

"Hardly. My, what a pity he ever sold the place.
Maybe it was getting too much for him, but still—"

"I was against it, but you know what he's like
when his mind's made up. He said a man of his age
ought to be able to afford to retire. He thought he'd
been in hardware long enough." Then Aunt Edna
laughed. "Hardware—that was certainly the right
thing for him to go into, wasn't it? Can you imagine
him in software or—heaven forbid—perishables?"

"Is there such a thing as software?" my mother
asked.

"Not in his language, kiddo," Aunt Edna said.

Then they both giggled, and I, all at once wanting
to be included, dropped my camouflage of silence.

"Why does Grandfather always say 'I seen' and
'I done'? Doesn't he know?"

Aunt Edna laughed again, but my mother did
not.

"Because he never had your advantages, young
lady, that's why," she said crossly. "He had to leave

school when he was just a child. Don't you ever mention it to him, either, do you hear? At least he doesn't say 'guy,' like some people I could name."

"Haw haw," I said sarcastically, but I said it very quietly so she did not hear.

"Nessa," Aunt Edna said, "where's that clothespeg doll you were making?"

I had forgotten it. I got it out now and decided I would be able to finish it today. Everyone else in Manawaka used the metal-spring type of clothespegs, but my grandmother still stuck to the all-wooden ones with a round knob on top and two straight legs. They were perfect for making dolls, and I used a pipe cleaner for the arms and bits of coloured crepe-paper for the clothes. This one was going to be an old-fashioned lady.

"You know, Beth," Aunt Edna said, "that's not right about advantages. He had plenty. Anyone could make a go of it in those days, if they were willing to work."

"Oh, I suppose so," my mother said. Her voice sounded peculiar, as though she were ashamed that she had brought the subject up. She turned away and bent her dark head over the big woodstove that said "McClary's Range" in shining script across the warming oven at the top. She poked at the bubbling cauliflower with a fork.

"I'll bet a nickel Ewen won't be back in time for dinner. It's Henry Pearl, and I guess he's in a pretty bad way, poor old fellow. He wouldn't come in to the hospital. He said he wants to die on his own place. Ewen won't get a cent, of course, but let's hope they pay in chickens this time, not that awful pork again, just loaded with fat."

"Why don't you ask me if I'd had any word?" Aunt Edna said coldly. "Since that's what you're wondering."

"Well, have you?"

"No. The ad's been in the Winnipeg papers for

the full two weeks now. Tell Ewen thanks but I'm afraid the money was wasted."

"If you think it would be any use, maybe we could—"

"No," my aunt said. "I'm not borrowing any more from Ewen. The two of you have enough to worry about."

"Well, maybe Winnipeg's not the right place to try. Maybe you'd have a better chance right here in Manawaka."

"Oh lord, Beth, don't you think I've gone to every office in town? They've all got stenographers already, for pity's sake, or else they can't afford to hire one. Won't this damn Depression ever be over? I can see myself staying on and on here in this house—"

I had put too much mucilage on the crepe-paper, and the pieces of the lady's skirt were slithering and refused to stick properly on the doll. Then half the skirt got stuck on my hand, and when I angrily yanked it away, the paper tore.

"Darn it! Darn this darned old thing!"

"What's the matter?" my mother asked.

"It won't stick, and now it's ripped. See? Now I'll have to cut out another skirt."

I grabbed the scissors and began hacking at another piece of paper.

"Well, as your grandmother says, there's no use getting in a fantod about it," my mother said. "Why don't you leave it now and go back to it when you're not so worked up?"

"No. I want to finish it today, and I'm going to."

It had become, somehow, overwhelmingly important for me to finish it. I did not even play with dolls very much, but this one was the beginning of a collection I had planned. I could visualise them, each dressed elaborately in the costume of some historical period or some distant country, ladies in hoop skirts, gents in black top hats, Highlanders in kilts, hula girls with necklaces of paper flowers. But this one did not

11

Gramley Library
Salem College
Winston-Salem, NC 27108

look at all as I had imagined she would. Her wooden face, on which I had already pencilled eyes and mouth, grinned stupidly at me, and I leered viciously back. *You'll be beautiful whether you like it or not,* I told her.

Aunt Edna hardly appeared to have noticed the interruption, but my mother had her eyes fixed dubiously on me, and I wished I had kept quiet.

"You know what he said yesterday?" Aunt Edna went on. "He told me I was almost as good as Jenny— she was their last hired girl, remember? Not as good, mark you. Almost."

"You mustn't be so touchy," my mother said. "He meant it as a compliment."

"I know," Aunt Edna said in a strained voice. "That's the hilarious part. Oh, Beth—"

"Nessa, honey," my mother said hastily, "run in and see if Grandmother wants to wait dinner for Daddy or not, will you?"

Humiliated and furious, I climbed down from the stool. She reached out to ruffle my hair in an apologetic gesture, but I brushed away her hand and walked into the living room, wrapped in my cloak of sullen haughtiness.

Grandfather was walking up and down in front of the bay window, first looking out and then consulting his pocket watch. He stared at me, and I hesitated. His eyes were the same Irish blue we all had, but the song "When Irish Eyes Are Smiling" had certainly not been referring to him.

"Where's your father got to, Vanessa?" he said. "He better get a move on."

Exhilarated with an accumulation of anger, I looked for something offensive to say.

"It's not his fault," I replied hotly. "It's Mr. Pearl. He's dying with pneumonia. I'll bet you he's spitting up blood this very second."

Did people spit blood with pneumonia? All at once, I could not swallow, feeling as though that gushing crimson were constricting my own throat. Something like that would go well in the story I was currently making up. *Sick to death in the freezing log cabin, with only the beautiful halfbreed lady* (no, *woman*) *to look after him, Old Jebb suddenly clutched his throat*—and so on.

"You mind how you talk," Grandfather was saying severely. "Do you want to upset your grandmother?"

This was a telling blow. I did not want to upset my grandmother. It was tacitly understood among all members of the family that Grandmother was not to be upset. Only Grandfather was allowed to upset her. The rest of us coddled her gladly, assuming that she needed protection. I looked guiltily at her now, but she appeared unaware that anything nasty had been spoken. If it had been a week-day, she would have been knitting an afghan, but as it was Sunday she was reading the Bible with the aid of a magnifying glass. She did not believe in eyeglasses, which were, she thought, unnatural. She did not believe in smoking or drinking or the playing of cards, either, but she never pushed her beliefs at other people nor made any claims for her own goodness. If a visitor lit up a cigarette, she did not say a word, not even after he had gone. This was not a question of piety to her, but of manners. She kept one ashtray in the house, for the use of smoking guests. It was a thick glass one, and it said in gilt letters "Queen Victoria Hotel, Manawaka." Uncle Terence, the second oldest of her children, had swiped it once, out of the hotel beer parlour, but Grandmother never knew that, and she was always under the impression that the management had given it to him for some reason or other, possibly because he must have been such a polite and considerate dining room guest, which was the only part of the hotel she thought he had ever been into.

My grandmother was a Mitigated Baptist. I knew this because I had heard my father say, "At least she's not an unmitigated Baptist," and when I enquired, he told me that if you were Unmitigated you believed in

Total Immersion, which meant that when you were baptised you had to be dunked in the Wachakwa River with all your clothes on. Unlike the United Church, where I went with my parents and where the baptisms were usually of newborn babies and the event happened only once for each person, in my grandmother's church the ritual was often performed with adults and could occur seasonally, if the call came. Grandmother had never plunged into the muddy Wachakwa.

"With her tendency to pleurisy," my father had said, "we can count it a singular blessing that your grandmother believes in font baptism."

Grandfather had started out a Methodist, but when the Methodists joined with the Presbyterians to form the United Church, he had refused to go because he did not like all the Scots who were now in the congregation. He had therefore turned Baptist and now went to Grandmother's church.

"It's a wonder he didn't join the Salvation Army," I had once heard Aunt Edna remark, "rather than follow her lead."

"Now, Edna," my mother had said, glancing sideways at me. So I heard nothing more of any interest that day, but I did not really care, for I was planning in my head a story in which an infant was baptised by Total Immersion and swept away by the river which happened to be flooding. (Why would it be flooding? Well, probably the spring ice was just melting. Would they do baptisms at that time of year? The water would be awfully cold. Obviously, some details needed to be worked out here.) The child was dressed in a christening robe of white lace, and the last the mother saw of her was a scrap of white being swirled away towards the Deep Hole near the Wachakwa bend, where there were blood-suckers.

Grandfather did not believe, either, in smoking, drinking, card-playing, dancing, or tobacco-chewing. But unlike my grandmother, he did not permit any of these things in his presence. If someone coming to the

Brick House for the first time chanced to light a cigarette when Grandfather was home, he gave them one chance and that was all. His warning was straightforward. He would walk to the front door, fling it open, and begin coughing. He would then say, "Smoky in here, ain't it?" If this had no effect, he told the visitor to get out, and no two ways about it. Aunt Edna once asked me to guess how many boyfriends she had lost that way, and when I said "I give up—how many?" she said "Five, and that's the gospel truth." At the time I imagined, because she was laughing, that she thought it was funny.

Grandfather had stopped his pacing now, and stood squarely in front of Grandmother's chair.

"Agnes, go and tell them girls to serve up the dinner now. We can't wait around all night."

"Will you go pet?" Grandmother said to me. "Your feet are younger than mine."

When I conveyed the message, Aunt Edna stood in the kitchen doorway and bellowed loud enough for a person to hear in South Wachakwa.

"Tell him the cauliflower isn't done yet!"

"Edna!" my mother hissed. Then she began laughing, and put her handkerchief over her face. I was laughing, too, until I looked again and saw that my mother was now crying, in jerky uncertain breaths like a person takes when he first goes outside in forty-below weather.

"Beth—" Swiftly, Aunt Edna had closed the kitchen door.

"I'm sorry," my mother said. "What an idiot. There —I'm fine now."

"Come on—we'll go up to my room and have a cigarette. Glory! What are we going to do when the Attar of Roses is all gone?"

The Attar of Roses was a decidedly strong-smelling perfume that had been given to Aunt Edna by one of her boyfriends in Winnipeg. It was in an atomiser, and she used to squirt it around her bedroom after she had finished a cigarette. On these occasions, my̆ mŏther always said, "Do you think we are teaching the child deception?" And Aunt Edna always replied, "No, just self-preservation."

I went up the back stairs with them. Aunt Edna's room had a white vanity table with thin legs and a mirror that could be turned this way and that. Beside the mirror sat a dresser doll that had been given to Aunt Edna by another admirer. "An old boyfriend," she had told me, and now that I was ten I understood that this did not refer to his age but to the fact that they were irrevocably parted, he being in the city and she in Manawaka. The doll had a china head and body, set on a wire hoop-skirt frame that was covered with fluted apricot *crêpe de chine*. Her high coiffure was fashioned of yellow curls, real hair cut from a real person's head. "Probably somebody that died of typhoid," Aunt Edna had said. "Well, *toujours gai*, kid, but I wish he had sent chocolates instead." Aunt Edna's room also had a blue silk eiderdown stuffed with duck feathers, a Japanese lacquer box with a picture of a chalk-faced oriental lady holding a fan, a camphor-ice in a tubular wooden case with a bulb head painted like a clown, a green leather jewellery case full of beads and earrings, and a floppy pyjama-bag doll embroidered with mysterious words such as "Immy-Jay" and "Oy-Ray" which I, like Grandmother, had believed were either meaningless or else Chinese, until I became acquainted with Pig Latin.

My mother sat down on the bed and Aunt Edna sat at the vanity table and began combing her hair. The smoke from their cigarettes made blue whorls in the air.

"Honey, what is it?" Aunt Edna asked in a worried voice.

"It's nothing," my mother said. "I'm not myself these days."

"You look worn out," Aunt Edna said. "Can't you quit the office? You'll have to, soon, anyway."

"I want to keep on as long as I can. Ewen can't afford to hire a nurse, Edna, you know that."

"Well, at least you needn't do your spring house-cleaning this year. Beating the carpet like you were doing last week—you're out of your head, Beth."

"The house is a disgrace," my mother said in a small voice. "I just want to get the rugs and curtains done, and the cupboards, that's all. I don't intend to do another thing."

"I'll bet," Aunt Edna said.

"Well, what about you?" my mother said. "Don't think I didn't notice you'd done the pantry cupboards this week. This house is far too much for you, Edna."

"Mother ran it, all those years."

"She had us to help, don't forget. And she was hardly ever without a hired girl."

"The least I can do is earn my room and board," Aunt Edna said. "I'm not going to have him saying—"

She broke off. My mother got up and put an arm around Aunt Edna's shoulder.

"There now, love. It's all right. It's going to be all right."

The phone rang, and I ran down to answer it, feeling some unaccustomed obligation. Their sadness was such a new thing, not to my actual sight but to my attention, that I felt it as bodily hurt, like skinning a knee, a sharp stinging pain. But I felt as well an obscure sense of loss. Some comfort had been taken from me, but I did not know what it was.

"Hello." It was Central's voice. She had a name, but no one in Manawaka ever called her anything except Central. "Is that you, Vanessa? Your dad's calling from South Wachakwa."

I heard a buzzing, and then my father's voice. "Vanessa? Listen, sweetheart, tell your mother I won't be home for a while yet. I'll have dinner here. And tell her she's to go home early and get to bed. How is she?"

"She's okay." But I was immediately alert. "Why? What was the matter with her?"

"Nothing. But you be sure to tell her, eh?"

I ran upstairs and repeated what he had said. Aunt Edna looked at my mother oddly.

"Beth?"

"It wasn't anything," my mother said quickly. "Only the merest speck. You know how Ewen fusses."

"No, he doesn't," Aunt Edna said. "You tell me the truth this minute, Beth."

My mother's voice was slow and without expression.

"All right, then. It was a pretty near thing, I suppose. It happened on Tuesday, after I'd been doing the rugs. That's why I didn't want to tell you. You don't need to say it was my own fault. I know it. But I'd been feeling perfectly well, Edna. Really I had."

She looked up at Aunt Edna, and there was something in her eyes I had not seen before, some mute appeal.

"If I'd lost it, I'd never have forgiven myself. I didn't do it on purpose, Edna."

"You don't have to tell me that," Aunt Edna cried. "Don't you think I know?"

And then, strangely, while I sat on the cedar chest and watched, only partially knowing and yet bound somehow to them, they hugged each other tightly and I saw the tears on both their faces although they were not making a sound.

"Mercy," my mother said at last, "my nose is shining like a beacon—where's your powder?"

When my mother had gone down to start serving the dinner, Aunt Edna put away the ashtrays and began spraying Attar of Roses around the room.

"How's the poetry?" she asked.

I was not shy about replying, for I loved to talk about myself. "I'm not doing any right now. I'm writing a story. I've filled two scribblers already."

"Oh?" Aunt Edna sounded impressed. "What are you calling it?"

"*The Pillars of the Nation*," I replied. "It's about pioneers."

"You mean—people like Grandfather?"

18

"My gosh," I said, startled. "Was he a pioneer?"

Then I felt awkward and at a distance from her, for she began to laugh hoarsely.

"I'll tell the cockeyed world," she said. Seeing I was offended, she cut off her laughter. "When do you work at it, Nessa?"

"After school, mostly. But sometimes at night."

"Does your mother let you keep your light on?"

I looked at her doubtfully, not sure how far she could be trusted. "If I tell you something, will you promise not to tell?"

"Cross my heart," she said, "and hope to die."

"I don't keep my light on. I use my flashlight."

"Mercy, what devotion. Do you write some every day?"

"Yes, every day," I said proudly.

"Couldn't you spin it out? Make it last longer?"

"I want to get it finished."

"Why? What's the rush?"

I was beginning to feel restless and suspicious.

"I don't know. I just want to get it done. I like doing it."

Aunt Edna put the perfume atomiser back on the vanity table.

"Sure, I know," she said. "But what if you ever wanted to stop, for a change?"

As we were going down the back stairs, we heard the front door open, and Grandfather's voice saying, "Well now, well now—" and then another voice. Aunt Edna gasped.

"Don't tell me. Oh heavenly days it *is* Uncle Dan. Now all I need is somebody from the government coming and telling me I owe income tax."

"I thought you liked Uncle Dan," I said curiously.

"I do," Aunt Edna said, "but it's not a question of whether you like a person or not."

We emerged into the kitchen. My mother had stopped carving the pork and was standing with the silver knife in her hand, motionless.

"He's certainly had a few, judging from his voice,"

19

she said. "Why on earth does he do it? He knows perfectly well how much it upsets Mother."

"One of these days Father is going to tell him to get out," Aunt Edna said. "But I'd kind of hate to see that happen, wouldn't you?"

"He'll never do that. Blood is thicker than water as you may have heard Father mention a million times."

"That's not why he lets him come around," Aunt Edna said. "Seeing Uncle Dan reminds him how well he's done himself, that's all. Lord, I must stop this—I'm getting meaner every day."

"Well, I suppose we'd better go and say hello to the old fraud," my mother said. "He can have Ewen's place at the table."

Uncle Dan was Grandfather's brother, but he was not upright. He had a farm in the South Wachakwa Valley, but he never planted any crops. He raised horses, and spent most of his time travelling around the country, selling them. At least, he was supposed to be selling them, but Aunt Edna said he had horse-trading in his blood and couldn't resist swapping, so he usually came back to Manawaka with the same number of horses he had started out with, only they were different horses, and no money. He had never married. I liked him because he always carried brown hot-tasting humbugs in his pockets, usually covered with navy fluff from his coat, and he sang Irish songs. I liked him only when none of my friends were around to see, however. In the presence of the other kids, he embarrassed me. He was older than Grandfather, and he did not keep himself very clean. His serge trousers were polka-dotted with spilled food, and when his nose ran, he wiped it with a sweeping motion of his claw hand. He never cleaned his fingernails, although sometimes he brought out his jackknife and pared them, dropping the shavings on Grandmother's polished hardwood floor and causing her to utter the only phrase of protest she knew— "Now Dan, now

Dan—" Sometimes when I was downtown with him he walked and talked waveringly, and bought an Eskimo Pie for me and a packet of Sen-Sen for himself, and I was not meant to know why, but naturally I did, having among my friends several whose fathers or uncles were said to be downright no-good.

Uncle Dan was smaller than Grandfather, but his eyes were the same blue. They bore a vastly different expression, however. Uncle Dan's eyes hardly ever stopped laughing.

"Well, Dan, you're back," Grandfather said.

"I'm back, I'm back," Uncle Dan carolled. "Just got the niftiest black two-year-old you ever seen. Got him from old Burnside, over at Freehold. Swapped him that grey gelding of mine."

"No cash, I'll wager," Grandfather said.

"Well, now, Timothy, how've you been?" Uncle Dan cried, cannily changing the subject. "You're looking dandy."

"I'm well enough," Grandfather said. "Minding my own business. I sold the store, Dan."

"Yeh, you done that before I went away. Taking life easy, eh?"

Under her breath, Aunt Edna said, "Red rag to a bull—" and my mother said, "Shush."

"I keep busy," Grandfather said furiously. "Plenty to do around here, you know. Got two loads of poplar last week, and I'm splitting them for kindling. A man's got to keep busy. I got no use for them fellows who just sit around."

"Well, well, you'll have the biggest woodpile in Manawaka, I wouldn't doubt it for a second," Uncle Dan said in gay malice. "By jiminy, here's Vanessa. You've grown, macushla, and so you have, to be sure."

"Oh Glory," said Aunt Edna in a low voice. "Macushla, indeed."

"And Beth and Edna—" Uncle Dan cried. "By the Lord Harry, girls, you're getting more beautiful with each passing day!"

My mother, stifling a laugh, held out a hand. "Good to see you, Uncle Dan. We're just going to have dinner. Do you want to go up and wash?"

"In a minute. Where's Agnes?"

Grandmother had not come out into the front hall. She still sat in the living room. The Book was on her knee, but she was not reading. Uncle Dan swept her an unsteady bow.

"Hello, Dan," she said. Then, apparently without effort, as though she refused to set bounds to her courtesy, "It's nice to have you with us."

Uncle Dan's eyes stopped smiling and grew moist with self-sorrow. "Ah, no, it's you that's the nice one, to be sure, opening your door to an old man."

His voice quavered; he looked as though he might faint with sheer fragility.

"If he goes on like that," Aunt Edna whispered angrily, but unable to suppress a small belch of acid mirth, "I'm walking out, so help me."

"He'll be all right once he's had some food," my mother said.

Dinner was very entertaining, with Uncle Dan tucking his serviette in at his chin, and spilling gravy on the clean damask cloth, and burping openly and then saying, "Par'n me, as the fella says." He told jokes of the kind I was not supposed to understand and which in fact I did not understand but always pretended I had, by rude guffaws for which I was reproached. Grandfather kept saying, "Mind your language, Dan," or "Mind your elbow—that water tumbler's going over—there, what did I tell you?" My mother and Aunt Edna kept their heads down and ate hurriedly. After dinner, Grandfather and Uncle Dan settled down side by side on the chesterfield, while Grandmother sat in her golden-oak armchair. Uncle Dan drew out his pipe and the oilcloth roll of tobacco. Aunt Edna, gathering up the dishes, glanced into the living room and began muttering.

"That damn pipe of his. It reeks to high heaven."

"Grandfather never lets anyone else smoke," I said, "so why Uncle Dan?"

"Don't ask me." Aunt Edna shrugged. "It's one of life's mysteries. Maybe it's his present to Uncle Dan—the booby prize."

I went into the living room to wait until the dishes were stacked and ready to begin drying. Grandfather and Uncle Dan were chatting, after their fashion.

"We're neither of us as young as we used to be, Dan," said Grandfather, who specialized in clear but gloomy statements of this kind.

"Oh, I wouldn't say that," Uncle Dan replied, sucking at his pipe and sending up grey clouds like smoke signals. "I feel pretty near as good as ever."

"You don't look it," Grandfather said.

"What's that?"

"I said you don't look it. You're getting hard of hearing, Dan."

Uncle Dan puffed silently for a moment. Then, with deliberation, he removed the pipe from between his yellowed teeth and held it in his hands, stroking the briar bowl.

"Well, sir, maybe you're right, at that," he said reflectively. "I used to be able to hear a fly when he walked up the wall, but now I can only hear him when he rustles his wings."

I snickered, and Uncle Dan looked down at the footstool where I was perched.

"There's my girl," he said. "What about a song, to while the happy hours away?"

Not waiting for my agreement, he struck up at once, in a reedy old-man's voice, sometimes going off key, but sprightly nonetheless, tapping out the rhythm with one foot.

With the tootle of the flute and twiddle of the fiddle,
A-twirlin' in the middle like a herring on a griddle,
Up, down, hands around, crossing to the wall,
Oh, hadn't we the gaiety at Phil the Fluter's Ball!

I clapped, feeling traitorous, not daring to look at either of my grandparents. Uncle Dan, encouraged, sang "MacNamara's Band," in which he always put himself instead of MacNamara.

Oh, me name is Danny Connor, I'm the leader of the band,
Although we're few in number, we're the finest in the land—

He sang it very Irish, saying "foinest," and when he got to the line "And when we play at funerals we play the best of all," he winked at me and I winked back.

"Sing with me," he said, before the next song, but I shook my head. I could never sing in front of anybody, for I always thought I might sound foolish, and I could not bear to be laughed at.

Uncle Dan kept right on, and now he was really enjoying himself. He sang "Nell Flaherty's Drake" with great vigour, especially the part about the curse that's laid on the person who stole and ate the bird.

May his pig never grunt,
May his cat never hunt,
May a ghost ever haunt him at dead of the night,
May his hens never lay,
May his horse never neigh,
May his goat fly away like an old paper kite—

All at once Grandfather slapped his hand down hard on the arm of the chesterfield, making it wheeze.

"That's enough, now," he said.

Uncle Dan continued his singing.

"Enough!" Grandfather shouted. "Are you stone deaf, man?"

Uncle Dan stopped, looking perplexed.

"What's the trouble?"

"Sunday wouldn't make no difference to you,"

24

Grandfather said, "but you needn't forget where you are."

"Well, now, Timothy," Uncle Dan said, "you needn't be like that about it."

"I'll be any way I please, in my own house," Grandfather said.

I judged this to be the right moment for me to go to the kitchen and help with the dishes. Now the two old men would sit and argue, and Grandmother would have to listen to the thing that distressed her more than anything in this world—a scene, a disagreement in the family. I knew quite well what would happen. Grandmother would remain as outwardly placid as ever, but later in the evening she would go out to the kitchen and call Aunt Edna and say, "I wonder if you would have an aspirin handy, pet? I've a little headache." When she had gone back to the living room, Aunt Edna would say to no one in particular, "She's been sitting there for hours with a splitting head, I don't doubt." And then, if I was in luck, my aunt would turn to me and say, "C'mon, kiddo, let's drown our sorrows—what do you say to some fudge?"

The dishes had been started. Aunt Edna handed me a tea-towel.

"Let's not break our necks over them, eh?" she said, and I knew she wanted to dawdle so she would not have to go back into the living room. But we did not dawdle, for my mother was a fast washer and we had to keep up with her.

"Was Uncle Dan born in Ireland?" I asked, conversationally.

My mother and Aunt Edna both laughed.

"Mercy, no," Aunt Edna said. "The closest he ever got to Ireland was the vaudeville shows at the old Roxy—it burned down before you were born. He was born in Ontario, just like Grandfather. The way Uncle Dan talks isn't Irish—it's stage Irish. He's got it all down pat. Macushla. Begorra. He even sings rebel songs, and he a Protestant. It makes no earthly difference to him. He's phoney as a three-dollar bill. I really wonder why I like him so much."

"You always told me I was half Irish," I said reproachfully to my mother.

"Well, you are," she replied. "You're Scottish on your father's side. You take after the MacLeods as much as the Connors. You've got your father's reflectiveness. And in looks, you've got your Grandfather MacLeod's hands and ears—"

She looked at me, as though to make certain that these borrowed appendages were still there. The idea of inherited characteristics had always seemed odd to me, and when I was younger, I had thought that my Grandfather MacLeod, who died a year after I was born, must have spent the last twelve months of his life deaf and handless.

"You're Irish on my side," my mother continued. "Your grandfather's parents were born there. Do you remember Grandma Connor, Edna? She lived with us for the last few years before she died."

"Only vaguely," Aunt Edna said. "What was she like?"

"Oh, let's see—she was a tiny little woman with a face like a falcon, as I recall, kind of fiercely handsome. Father looks quite a bit like her. She used to go out each year to the Orangemen's parade, and stand there on Main, cheering and bawling her eyes out."

"My Lord," Aunt Edna said. "What did Father think of that?"

"He was mortified," my mother said. "Wouldn't you be? There was this small ferocious old lady, making a regular spectacle of herself. She always wore a tight lace cap on her head. She didn't have any hair."

"What?" Aunt Edna and I cried at the same time, delighted and horrified.

My mother nodded. "It's quite true. She'd had some sickness and all her hair fell out. She was bald as a peeled onion."

We were still laughing when we heard the shouting from the living room. I found it hard to switch mood suddenly, and could not take the raised voices seriously. Tittering, I nudged my mother, wanting the shared hilarity to continue. She did not respond, and when I looked up at her, I saw her face was rigid and apprehensive. The joke was over as though it had never been. My mother and my aunt went reluctantly into the living room, and I followed.

"What beats me," Grandfather was saying, "is how you'd the nerve to ask. Easy come, easy go—that's what you think. It never come easy to me, and it's not going easy, neither!"

"Steady, Timothy," Uncle Dan said, as though he were speaking to a horse that had turned mean. "Steady, boyo."

"Steady, nothing. You think because I sold the store that I've got a fortune stowed away. Well, I've not. And what I've got, I'm hanging on to. The taxes on this house alone—it don't bear thinking about. Who's to look after things, if I don't? Here's Edna, keeps claiming she can't get work. And Beth and Ewen, having another baby they've no business to be having if Ewen can't even get people to pay their doctor bills. I'd make them pay up, I'll tell the world, either that or I'd stay away from the woman entirely—"

"Oh God—" my mother said, her face white.

"Steady," Aunt Edna said, grasping her by the arm.

"And now you," Grandfather went on. "All of you, picking away, picking away, wanting something for nothing. I never got it for nothing. None of you know that. Not one of you knows it."

"Hold on a minute," Uncle Dan protested. "I never said give, I said lend. You'd have the horses for security. You done it before, Tim."

"The more fool I, then," Grandfather retorted. "I hoped you'd make a go of things. But no. It all went up in smoke or down in booze."

"That ain't true!" Uncle Dan said.

But there was something feeble about his voice. And I realised that it was true, what Grandfather had said.

"No use in talking," Grandfather said. "You can get out right now."

In the long silence, I looked at my grandfather's face. He looked surprised, as though he could hardly believe he had spoken the words. Then his expression altered, grew set and stubborn.

"I will," Uncle Dan said slowly, "and I'll not be coming back."

"So much the better," Grandfather said.

Uncle Dan rose, walked out to the hall alone, and began putting on his coat.

"We can't let him go like that," Aunt Edna whispered. "He's got no one—"

"Who's going to argue it?" my mother replied bitterly.

The front door closed behind Uncle Dan, and everyone in the house stood quite still. Then a very unexpected thing happened.

"Timothy," Grandmother said, "you'd best go after him."

Grandfather swung around and stared at her.

"You're out of your mind," he said.

"You'd best go now," Grandmother said firmly, "before he gets too far."

For a moment I thought Grandfather was going to rage again, but he did not. He looked taken aback, almost stunned.

"You never liked his ways, Agnes," he said.

Grandmother did not reply. She made a slight gesture towards the door, and that was all. *How are the mighty fallen in the midst of the battle.* The line slid stealthily into my mind, and I felt a surge of spiteful joy at it. Then I looked again at my grandfather's face, and saw there such a bleak bewilderment that I could feel only shame and sadness. His eyes chanced upon me, and when he spoke it was to me, as though he could not speak directly to any of the adults in that room.

"When he gets too old to look after himself, it'll be me that pays to have him kept in a home. It's not fair, Vanessa. It's not fair."

He was right. It was not fair. Even I could see that. Yet I veered sharply away from his touch, and that was probably not fair, either. I wanted only to be by myself, with no one else around.

Grandfather turned and looked at Grandmother.

"I never thought to hear you take his part," he said.

Then he walked outside and we heard his flat unemphatic voice, speaking Uncle Dan's name.

When Uncle Dan and Grandfather had come back to the living room, the three old people settled down once more and sat silently in the blue-grey light of the spring evening, the lamps not flicked on yet nor the shades drawn. I went upstairs with my mother and Aunt Edna. The air in the bedroom was still sweet and heavy with Attar of Roses.

"Mercy, do I ever need a cigarette," Aunt Edna said.

"If I didn't know Mother better, I'd say it was revenge," my mother said.

"Know her? What makes you think you know her? Maybe it was just that."

"Maybe," my mother said, "but I'd hate to think so, wouldn't you?"

"No," my aunt said. "I'd cheer like sixty."

"Anyway, there's more to it than that," my mother said. "We always just naturally assumed she loathed the sight of Uncle Dan, but she said to me once, 'Whatever his faults, he's a cheerful soul, Beth, always remember that.' I'd forgotten until now."

"Beth, do you think she ever considered marrying him?"

"What? Mother? Don't be ridiculous. What makes you say that?"

"Remember how Uncle Dan used to take us out in that cutter of his in winter, when we were kids? Mother always worried in case we got dumped in a snowdrift or the horses ran away. Well, I went out once with him, and out of a clear sky he said 'She picked the right man, Edna, your mother, no question of it.' That was a funny thing for him to say, wasn't it?"

"I don't suppose it meant anything," my mother said.

"I wonder, though," Aunt Edna mused, "what all of us would have been like, if she'd—"

"A pretty ragged bunch," my mother said. "There's not much doubt about that. Oh Edna, think how he must feel—Father, I mean. We've never given him credit for what he's done."

"I wouldn't say that," Aunt Edna said. "Imitation is the sincerest form of compliment, after all."

My mother's head came up and she looked around this way and that, as though she smelled smoke and thought the house might be on fire.

"What do you mean by that?"

"You know quite well what I mean," Aunt Edna replied. "Not one of us could go any other way. And what's more, for all you're always saying Vanessa takes after Ewen, you know who she really takes after."

"That's not so!" my mother burst out.

"Isn't it?" Aunt Edna cried. "Isn't it?"

I was hardly aware of her meaning. I was going instead by the feel of the words, the same way the faithful must interpret the utterances of those who rise up and speak in tongues. Her voice was high and fearful, burdened with a terrible regret, as though she would have given anything not to have spoken.

We went downstairs then, and I helped to pass the coffee around, walking carefully because it was in the good Spode cups. Grandfather and Uncle Dan took theirs without a word. Grandmother said, "Thank you, pet." Her face was calm, and no one could even have begun to guess, from looking at her, what she might have been thinking, if anything. When he had finished his coffee, Uncle Dan said he thought he would just stroll down to the Regal Café and get a few humbugs.

My mother, coming in with the coffee pot to see if anyone wanted a second cup, hesitated and looked from Uncle Dan to Grandfather, as though she didn't know which of them to ask and couldn't ask both of them at once. Finally she sighed, a mere breath, and refilled Grandfather's cup. Uncle Dan went out, humming softly to himself, and when he had reached the front sidewalk he began to sing. We heard the song growing fainter as he ambled away.

> *Glory-o, Glory-o,*
> *To the bold Fenian men—*

Aunt Edna smothered a laugh. "Fenian! Grandma Connor would have a fit!"

My mother suddenly put a hand out and touched me lightly on the shoulder.

"Go with him, Vanessa," she said. "Keep him company."

And I ran, ran towards the sound of the singing. But he seemed a long way off now, and I wondered if I would ever catch up to him.

To Set Our House in Order

When the baby was almost ready to be born, something went wrong and my mother had to go into hospital two weeks before the expected time. I was wakened by her crying in the night, and then I heard my father's footsteps as he went downstairs to phone. I stood in the doorway of my room, shivering and listening, wanting to go to my mother but afraid to go lest there be some sight there more terrifying than I could bear.

"Hello—Paul?" my father said, and I knew he was talking to Dr. Cates. "It's Beth. The waters have broken, and the fetal position doesn't seem quite—well, I'm only thinking of what happened the last time, and another like that would be—I wish she were a little huskier, damn it—she's so—no, don't worry, I'm quite all right. Yes, I think that would be the best thing. Okay, make it as soon as you can, will you?"

He came back upstairs, looking bony and dishevelled in his pyjamas, and running his fingers through his sand-coloured hair. At the top of the stairs, he came face to face with Grandmother MacLeod, who was standing there in her quilted black satin dressing gown, her slight figure held straight and poised, as though she were unaware that her hair was bound grotesquely like white-feathered wings in the snare of her coarse night-time hairnet.

"What is it, Ewen?"

"It's all right, Mother. Beth's having—a little

trouble. I'm going to take her into the hospital. You go back to bed."

"I told you," Grandmother MacLeod said in her clear voice, never loud, but distinct and ringing like the tap of a sterling teaspoon on a crystal goblet, "I did tell you, Ewen, did I not, that you should have got a girl in to help her with the housework? She would have rested more."

"I couldn't afford to get anyone in," my father said. "If you thought she should've rested more, why didn't you ever—oh God, I'm out of my mind to-night—just go back to bed, Mother, please. I must get back to Beth."

When my father went down to the front door to let Dr. Cates in, my need overcame my fear and I slipped into my parents' room. My mother's black hair, so neatly pinned up during the day, was startlingly spread across the white pillowcase. I stared at her, not speaking, and then she smiled and I rushed from the doorway and buried my head upon her.

"It's all right, honey," she said. "Listen, Vanessa, the baby's just going to come a little early, that's all. You'll be all right. Grandmother MacLeod will be here."

"How can she get the meals?" I wailed, fixing on the first thing that came to mind. "She never cooks. She doesn't know how."

"Yes, she does," my mother said. "She can cook as well as anyone when she has to. She's just never had to very much, that's all. Don't worry—she'll keep everything in order, and then some."

My father and Dr. Cates came in, and I had to go, without ever saying anything I had wanted to say. I went back to my own room and lay with the shadows all around me. I listened to the night murmurings that always went on in that house, sounds which never had a source, rafters and beams contracting in the dry air, perhaps, or mice in the walls, or a sparrow that had flown into the attic

33

through the broken skylight there. After a while, although I would not have believed it possible, I slept.

The next morning I questioned my father. I believed him to be not only the best doctor in Manawaka, but also the best doctor in the whole of Manitoba, if not in the entire world, and the fact that he was not the one who was looking after my mother seemed to have something sinister about it.

"But it's always done that way, Vanessa," he explained. "Doctors never attend members of their own family. It's because they care so much about them, you see, and—"

"And what?" I insisted, alarmed at the way he had broken off. But my father did not reply. He stood there, and then he put on that difficult smile with which adults seek to conceal pain from children. I felt terrified, and ran to him, and he held me tightly.

"She's going to be fine," he said. "Honestly she is. Nessa, don't cry—"

Grandmother MacLeod appeared beside us, steel-spined despite her apparent fragility. She was wearing a purple silk dress and her ivory pendant. She looked as though she were all ready to go out for afternoon tea.

"Ewen, you're only encouraging the child to give way," she said. "Vanessa, big girls of ten don't make such a fuss about things. Come and get your breakfast. Now, Ewen, you're not to worry. I'll see to everything."

Summer holidays were not quite over, but I did not feel like going out to play with any of the kids. I was very superstitious, and I had the feeling that if I left the house, even for a few hours, some disaster would overtake my mother. I did not, of course, mention this feeling to Grandmother MacLeod, for she did not believe in the existence of fear, or if she did, she never let on. I spent the morning morbidly, in seeking hidden places in the house. There were many of these—odd-shaped nooks under the stairs, small and loosely nailed-up doors at the back of clothes closets, leading to dusty tunnels and forgotten recesses in the heart of the house where the only things actually to be seen were drab oil paintings stacked upon the rafters, and trunks full of outmoded clothing and old photograph albums. But the unseen presences in these secret places I knew to be those of every person, young or old, who had ever belonged to the house and had died, including Uncle Roderick who got killed on the Somme, and the baby who would have been my sister if only she had managed to come to life. Grandfather MacLeod, who had died a year after I was born, was present in the house in more tangible form. At the top of the main stairs hung the mammoth picture of a darkly uniformed man riding upon a horse whose prancing stance and dilated nostrils suggested that the battle was not yet over, that it might indeed continue until Judgment Day. The stern man was actually the Duke of Wellington, but at the time I believed him to be my grandfather MacLeod, still keeping an eye on things.

We had moved in with Grandmother MacLeod when the Depression got bad and she could no longer afford a housekeeper, but the MacLeod house never seemed like home to me. Its dark red brick was grown over at the front with Virginia creeper that turned crimson in the fall, until you could hardly tell brick from leaves. It boasted a small tower in which Grandmother MacLeod kept a weedy collection of anaemic ferns. The verandah was embellished with a profusion of wrought-iron scrolls, and the circular rose-window upstairs contained glass of many colours which permitted an outlooking eye to see the world as a place of absolute sapphire or emerald, or if one wished to look with a jaundiced eye, a hateful yellow. In Grandmother MacLeod's opinion, these features gave the house style.

Inside, a multitude of doors led to rooms where my presence, if not actually forbidden, was not encouraged. One was Grandmother MacLeod's bedroom, with its stale and old-smelling air, the dim reek of medicines and lavender sachets. Here resided her monogrammed dresser silver, brush and mirror, nail-buffer and button hook and scissors, none of which must even be fingered by me now, for she meant to leave them to me in her will and intended to hand them over in the same flawless and unused condition in which they had always been kept. Here, too, were the silver-framed photographs of Uncle Roderick—as a child, as a boy, as a man in his Army uniform. The massive walnut spool bed had obviously been designed for queens or giants, and my tiny grandmother used to lie within it all day when she had migraine, contriving somehow to look like a giant queen.

The living room was another alien territory where I had to tread warily, for many valuable objects sat just-so on tables and mantelpiece, and dirt must not be tracked in upon the blue Chinese carpet with its birds in eternal motionless flight and its water-lily buds caught forever just before the point of opening. My mother was always nervous when I was in this room.

"Vanessa, honey," she would say, half apologetically, "why don't you go and play in the den, or upstairs?"

"Can't you leave her, Beth?" my father would say. "She's not doing any harm."

"I'm only thinking of the rug," my mother would say, glancing at Grandmother MacLeod, "and yesterday she nearly knocked the Dresden shepherdess off the mantel. I mean, she can't help it, Ewen, she has to run around—"

"Goddamn it, I know she can't help it," my father would growl, glaring at the smirking face of the Dresden shepherdess.

"I see no need to blaspheme, Ewen," Grandmother MacLeod would say quietly, and then my father would say he was sorry, and I would leave.

The day my mother went to the hospital, Grandmother MacLeod called me at lunch-time, and when I appeared, smudged with dust from the attic, she looked at me distastefully as though I had been a cockroach that had just crawled impertinently out of the woodwork.

"For mercy's sake, Vanessa, what have you been doing with yourself? Run and get washed this minute. Here, not that way—you use the back stairs, young lady. Get along now. Oh—your father phoned."

I swung around. "What did he say? How is she? Is the baby born?"

"Curiosity killed a cat," Grandmother MacLeod said, frowning. "I cannot understand Beth and Ewen telling you all these things, at your age. What sort of vulgar person you'll grow up to be, I dare not think. No, it's not born yet. Your mother's just the same. No change."

I looked at my grandmother, not wanting to appeal to her, but unable to stop myself. "Will she—will she be all right?"

Grandmother MacLeod straightened her already-straight back. "If I said definitely yes, Vanessa, that would be a lie, and the MacLeods do not tell lies, as I have tried to impress upon you before. What happens is God's will. The Lord giveth, and the Lord taketh away."

Appalled, I turned away so she would not see my face and my eyes. Surprisingly, I heard her sigh and felt her papery white and perfectly manicured hand upon my shoulder.

"When your Uncle Roderick got killed," she said, "I thought I would die. But I didn't die, Vanessa."

At lunch, she chatted animatedly, and I realised she was trying to cheer me in the only way she knew.

"When I married your Grandfather MacLeod," she related, "he said to me, 'Eleanor, don't think because we're going to the prairies that I expect you to live roughly. You're used to a proper house, and you shall have one.' He was as good as his word. Before we'd been in Manawaka three years, he'd had this place built. He earned a good deal of money in his time, your grandfather. He soon had more patients than either of the other doctors. We ordered our dinner service and all our silver from Birks' in Toronto. We had resident help in those days, of course, and never had less than twelve guests for dinner parties. When I had a tea, it would always be twenty or thirty. Never any less than half a dozen different kinds of cake were ever served in this house. Well, no one seems to bother much these days. Too lazy, I suppose."

"Too broke," I suggested. "That's what Dad says."

"I can't bear slang," Grandmother MacLeod said. "If you mean hard up, why don't you say so? It's mainly a question of management, anyway. My accounts were always in good order, and so was my house. No unexpected expenses that couldn't be met, no fruit cellar running out of preserves before the winter was over. Do you know what my father used to say to me when I was a girl?"

"No," I said. "What?"

"God loves Order," Grandmother MacLeod replied with emphasis. "You remember that, Vanessa. God loves Order—he wants each one of us to set our house in order. I've never forgotten those words of my father's. I was a MacInnes before I got married. The MacInnes is a very ancient clan, the lairds of Morven and the constables of the Castle of Kinlochaline. Did you finish that book I gave you?"

"Yes," I said. Then, feeling some additional comment to be called for, "It was a swell book, Grandmother."

This was somewhat short of the truth. I had been hoping for her cairngorm brooch on my tenth birthday, and had received instead the plaid-bound volume entitled *The Clans and Tartans of Scotland.* Most of it was too boring to read, but I had looked up the motto of my own family and those of some of my friends' families. *Be then a wall of brass. Learn to suffer. Consider the end. Go carefully.* I had not found any of these slogans reassuring. What with Mavis Duncan learning to suffer, and Laura Kennedy considering the end, and Patsy Drummond going carefully, and I spending my time in being a wall of brass, it did not seem to me that any of us were going to lead very interesting lives. I did not say this to Grandmother MacLeod.

"The MacInnes motto is *Pleasure Arises from Work*," I said.

"Yes," she agreed proudly. "And an excellent motto it is, too. One to bear in mind."

She rose from the table, rearranging on her bosom the looped ivory beads that held the pendant on which a fullblown ivory rose was stiffly carved.

"I hope Ewen will be pleased," she said.

"What at?"

"Didn't I tell you?" Grandmother MacLeod said. "I hired a girl this morning, for the housework. She's to start tomorrow."

When my father got home that evening, Grandmother MacLeod told him her good news. He ran one hand distractedly across his forehead.

"I'm sorry, Mother, but you'll just have to unhire her. I can't possibly pay anyone."

"It seems distinctly odd," Grandmother MacLeod snapped, "that you can afford to eat chicken four times a week."

"Those chickens," my father said in an exasperated voice, "are how people are paying their bills. The same with the eggs and the milk. That scrawny turkey that arrived yesterday was for Logan MacCardney's appendix, if you must know. We probably eat better than any family in Manawaka, except Niall Cameron's. People can't entirely dispense with doctors or undertakers. That doesn't mean to say I've got any cash. Look, Mother, I don't know what's happening with Beth. Paul thinks he may have to do a Caesarean. Can't we leave all this? Just leave the house alone. Don't touch it. What does it matter?"

"I have never lived in a messy house, Ewen," Grandmother MacLeod said, "and I don't intend to begin now."

"Oh Lord," my father said. "Well, I'll phone Edna, I guess, and see if she can give us a hand, although God knows she's got enough, with the Connor house and her parents to look after."

"I don't fancy having Edna Connor in to help," Grandmother MacLeod objected.

"Why not?" my father shouted. "She's Beth's sister, isn't she?"

"She speaks in such a slangy way," Grandmother MacLeod said. "I have never believed she was a good influence on Vanessa. And there is no need for you to raise your voice to me, Ewen, if you please."

I could barely control my rage. I thought my father would surely rise to Aunt Edna's defence. But he did not.

"It'll be all right," he soothed her. "She'd only be here for part of the day, Mother. You could stay in your room."

Aunt Edna strode in the next morning. The sight of her bobbed black hair and her grin made me feel better at once. She hauled out the carpet sweeper and the weighted polisher and got to work. I dusted while she polished and swept, and we got through the living room and front hall in next to no time.

"Where's her royal highness, kiddo?" she enquired.

"In her room," I said. "She's reading the catalogue from Robinson & Cleaver."

"Good Glory, not again?" Aunt Edna cried. "The last time she ordered three linen tea-cloths and two dozen serviettes. It came to fourteen dollars. Your mother was absolutely frantic. I guess I shouldn't be saying this."

"I knew anyway," I assured her. "She was at the lace handkerchiefs section when I took up her coffee."

"Let's hope she stays there. Heaven forbid she should get onto the banqueting cloths. Well, at least she believes the Irish are good for two things—manual labour and linen-making. She's never forgotten Father used to be a blacksmith, before he got the hardware store. Can you beat it? I wish it didn't bother Beth."

"Does it?" I asked, and immediately realised this was a wrong move, for Aunt Edna was suddenly scrutinising me.

"We're making you grow up before your time," she said. "Don't pay any attention to me, Nessa. I must've got up on the wrong side of the bed this morning."

But I was unwilling to leave the subject.

"All the same," I said thoughtfully, "Grandmother MacLeod's family were the lairds of Morven and the constables of the Castle of Kinlochaline. I bet you didn't know that."

Aunt Edna snorted. "Castle, my foot. She was born in Ontario, just like your Grandfather Connor, and her father was a horse doctor. Come on, kiddo, we'd better shut up and get down to business here."

We worked in silence for a while.

"Aunt Edna—" I said at last, "what about Mother? Why won't they let me go and see her?"

"Kids aren't allowed to visit maternity patients. It's tough for you, I know that. Look, Nessa, don't worry. If it doesn't start tonight, they're going to do the operation. She's getting the best of care."

I stood there, holding the feather duster like a dead bird in my hands. I was not aware that I was going to speak until the words came out.

"I'm scared," I said.

Aunt Edna put her arms around me, and her face looked all at once stricken and empty of defences.

"Oh, honey, I'm scared, too," she said.

It was this way that Grandmother MacLeod found us when she came stepping lightly down into the front hall with the order in her hand for two dozen lace-bordered handkerchiefs of pure Irish linen.

I could not sleep that night, and when I went downstairs, I found my father in the den. I sat down on the hassock beside his chair, and he told me about the operation my mother was to have the next morning. He kept on saying it was not serious nowadays.

"But you're worried," I put in, as though seeking to explain why I was.

"I should at least have been able to keep from burdening you with it," he said in a distant voice, as though to himself. "If only the baby hadn't got itself twisted around—"

"Will it be born dead, like the little girl?"

"I don't know," my father said. "I hope not."

"She'd be disappointed, wouldn't she, if it was?" I said bleakly, wondering why I was not enough for her.

"Yes, she would," my father replied. "She won't be able to have any more, after this. It's partly on your account that she wants this one, Nessa. She doesn't want you to grow up without a brother or sister."

"As far as I'm concerned, she didn't need to bother," I retorted angrily.

My father laughed. "Well, let's talk about something else, and then maybe you'll be able to sleep. How did you and Grandmother make out today?"

"Oh, fine, I guess. What was Grandfather MacLeod like, Dad?"

"What did she tell you about him?"

"She said he made a lot of money in his time."

"Well, he wasn't any millionaire," my father said, "but I suppose he did quite well. That's not what I associate with him, though."

He reached across to the bookshelf, took out a small leather-bound volume and opened it. On the pages were mysterious marks, like doodling, only much neater and more patterned.

"What is it?" I asked.

"Greek," my father explained. "This is a play called *Antigone*. See, here's the title in English. There's a whole stack of them on the shelves there. *Oedipus Rex. Electra. Medea.* They belonged to your Grandfather MacLeod. He used to read them often."

"Why?" I enquired, unable to understand why anyone would pore over those undecipherable signs.

"He was interested in them," my father said. "He must have been a lonely man, although it never struck me that way at the time. Sometimes a thing only hits you a long time afterwards."

"Why would he be lonely?" I wanted to know.

"He was the only person in Manawaka who could read these plays in the original Greek," my father said. "I don't suppose many people, if anyone, had even read them in English translations. Maybe he would have liked to be a classical scholar—I don't know. But his father was a doctor, so that's what he was. Maybe he would have liked to talk to somebody about these plays. They must have meant a lot to him."

It seemed to me that my father was talking oddly. There was a sadness in his voice that I had never heard before, and I longed to say something that would make him feel better, but I could not, because I did not know what was the matter.

"Can you read this kind of writing?" I asked hesitantly.

My father shook his head. "Nope. I was never very intellectual, I guess. Rod was always brighter than I, in school, but even he wasn't interested in learning Greek. Perhaps he would've been later, if he'd lived. As a kid, all I ever wanted to do was go into the merchant marine."

"Why didn't you, then?"

"Oh well," my father said offhandedly, "a kid who'd never seen the sea wouldn't have made much of a sailor. I might have turned out to be the seasick type."

I had lost interest now that he was speaking once more like himself.

"Grandmother MacLeod was pretty cross today about the girl," I remarked.

"I know," my father nodded. "Well, we must be as nice as we can to her, Nessa, and after a while she'll be all right."

Suddenly I did not care what I said.

"Why can't she be nice to us for a change?" I

burst out. "We're always the ones who have to be nice to her."

My father put his hand down and slowly tilted my head until I was forced to look at him.

"Vanessa," he said, "she's had troubles in her life which you really don't know much about. That's why she gets migraine sometimes and has to go to bed. It's not easy for her these days, either—the house is still the same, so she thinks other things should be, too. It hurts her when she finds they aren't."

"I don't see—" I began.

"Listen," my father said, "you know we were talking about what people are interested in, like Grandfather MacLeod being interested in Greek plays? Well, your grandmother was interested in being a lady, Nessa, and for a long time it seemed to her that she was one."

I thought of the Castle of Kinlochaline, and of horse doctors in Ontario.

"I didn't know—" I stammered.

"That's usually the trouble with most of us," my father said. "You go on up to bed now. I'll phone tomorrow from the hospital as soon as the operation's over."

I did sleep at last, and in my dreams I could hear the caught sparrow fluttering in the attic, and the sound of my mother crying, and the voices of the dead children.

My father did not phone until afternoon. Grandmother MacLeod said I was being silly, for you could hear the phone ringing all over the house, but nevertheless I refused to move out of the den. I had never before examined my father's books, but now, at a loss for something to do, I took them out one by one and read snatches here and there. After I had been doing this for several hours, it dawned on me that most of the books were of the same kind. I looked again at the titles.

Seven-League Boots. Arabia Deserta. The Seven Pillars of Wisdom. Travels in Tibet. Count Lucknor the Sea Devil. And a hundred more. On a shelf by themselves were copies of the *National Geographic* magazine, which I looked at often enough, but never before with the puzzling compulsion which I felt now, as though I were on the verge of some discovery, something which I had to find out and yet did not want to know. I riffled through the picture-filled pages. Hibiscus and wild orchids grew in a soft-petalled confusion. The Himalayas stood lofty as gods, with the morning sun on their peaks of snow. Leopards snarled from the vined depths of a thousand jungles. Schooners buffetted their white sails like the wings of giant angels against the great sea winds.

"What on earth are you doing?" Grandmother MacLeod enquired waspishly, from the doorway. "You've got everything scattered all over the place. Pick it all up this minute, Vanessa, do you hear?"

So I picked up the books and magazines, and put them all neatly away, as I had been told to do.

When the telephone finally rang, I was afraid to answer it. At last I picked it up. My father sounded faraway, and the relief in his voice made it unsteady.

"It's okay, honey. Everything's fine. The boy was born alive and kicking after all. Your mother's pretty weak, but she's going to be all right."

I could hardly believe it. I did not want to talk to anyone. I wanted to be by myself, to assimilate the presence of my brother, towards whom, without ever having seen him yet, I felt such tenderness and such resentment.

That evening, Grandmother MacLeod approached my father, who, still dazed with the unexpected gift of neither life now being threatened, at first did not take her seriously when she asked what they planned to call the child.

"Oh, I don't know. Hank, maybe, or Joe. Fauntleroy, perhaps."

She ignored his levity.

"Ewen," she said, "I wish you would call him Roderick."

My father's face changed. "I'd rather not."

"I think you should," Grandmother MacLeod insisted, very quietly, but in a voice as pointed and precise as her silver nail-scissors.

"Don't you think Beth ought to decide?" my father asked.

"Beth will agree if you do."

My father did not bother to deny something that even I knew to be true. He did not say anything. Then Grandmother MacLeod's voice, astonishingly, faltered a little.

"It would mean a great deal to me," she said.

I remembered what she had told me—*When your Uncle Roderick got killed, I thought I would die. But I didn't die.* All at once, her feeling for that unknown dead man became a reality for me. And yet I held it against her, as well, for I could see that it had enabled her to win now.

"All right," my father said tiredly. "We'll call him Roderick."

Then, alarmingly, he threw back his head and laughed.

"Roderick Dhu!" he cried. "That's what you'll call him, isn't it? Black Roderick. Like before. Don't you remember? As though he were a character out of Sir Walter Scott, instead of an ordinary kid who—"

He broke off, and looked at her with a kind of desolation in his face.

"God, I'm sorry, Mother," he said. "I had no right to say that."

Grandmother MacLeod did not flinch, or tremble, or indicate that she felt anything at all.

"I accept your apology, Ewen," she said.

My mother had to stay in bed for several weeks after she arrived home. The baby's cot was kept in my parents' room, and I could go in and look at the small

46

creature who lay there with his tightly closed fists and his feathery black hair. Aunt Edna came in to help each morning, and when she had finished the housework, she would have coffee with my mother. They kept the door closed, but this did not prevent me from eavesdropping, for there was an air register in the floor of the spare room, which was linked somehow with the register in my parents' room. If you put your ear to the iron grille, it was almost like a radio.

"Did you mind very much, Beth?" Aunt Edna was saying.

"Oh, it's not the name I mind," my mother replied. "It's just the fact that Ewen felt he had to. You know that Rod had only had the sight of one eye, didn't you?"

"Sure, I knew. So what?"

"There was only a year and a half between Ewen and Rod," my mother said, "so they often went around together when they were youngsters. It was Ewen's air-rifle that did it."

"Oh Lord," Aunt Edna said heavily. "I suppose she always blamed him?"

"No, I don't think it was so much that, really. It was how he felt himself. I think he even used to wonder sometimes if—but people shouldn't let themselves think like that, or they'd go crazy. Accidents do happen, after all. When the war came, Ewen joined up first. Rod should never have been in the Army at all, but he couldn't wait to get in. He must have lied about his eyesight. It wasn't so very noticeable unless you looked at him closely, and I don't suppose the medicals were very thorough in those days. He got in as a gunner, and Ewen applied to have him in the same company. He thought he might be able to watch out for him, I guess, Rod being—at a disadvantage. They were both only kids. Ewen was nineteen and Rod was eighteen when they went to France. And then the Somme. I don't know, Edna, I think Ewen felt that if Rod had had proper sight, or if he hadn't been in the same outfit and had been sent somewhere else—

you know how people always think these things afterwards, not that it's ever a bit of use. Ewen wasn't there when Rod got hit. They'd lost each other somehow, and Ewen was looking for him, not bothering about anything else, you know, just frantically looking. Then he stumbled across him quite by chance. Rod was still alive, but—"

"Stop it, Beth," Aunt Edna said. "You're only upsetting yourself."

"Ewen never spoke of it to me," my mother went on, "until once his mother showed me the letter he'd written to her at the time. It was a peculiar letter, almost formal, saying how gallantly Rod had died, and all that. I guess I shouldn't have, but I told him she'd shown it to me. He was very angry that she had. And then, as though for some reason he were terribly ashamed, he said—*I had to write something to her, but men don't really die like that, Beth. It wasn't that way at all.* It was only after the war that he decided to come back and study medicine and go into practice with his father."

"Had Rod meant to?" Aunt Edna asked.

"I don't know," my mother said slowly. "I never felt I should ask Ewen that."

Aunt Edna was gathering up the coffee things, for I could hear the clash of cups and saucers being stacked on the tray.

"You know what I heard her say to Vanessa once, Beth? *The MacLeods never tell lies.* Those were her exact words. Even then, I didn't know whether to laugh or cry."

"Please, Edna—" my mother sounded worn out now. "Don't."

"Oh Glory," Aunt Edna said remorsefully, "I've got all the delicacy of a two-ton truck. I didn't mean Ewen, for heaven's sake. That wasn't what I meant at all. Here, let me plump up your pillows for you."

Then the baby began to cry, so I could not hear anything more of interest. I took my bike and went out beyond Manawaka, riding aimlessly along the gravel highway. It was late summer, and the wheat had changed colour, but instead of being high and bronzed in the fields, it was stunted and desiccated, for there had been no rain again this year. But in the bluff where I stopped and crawled under the barbed wire fence and lay stretched out on the grass, the plentiful poplar leaves were turning to a luminous yellow and shone like church windows in the sun. I put my head down very close to the earth and looked at what was going on there. Grasshoppers with enormous eyes ticked and twitched around me, as though the dry air were perfect for their purposes. A ladybird laboured mightily to climb a blade of grass, fell off, and started all over again, seeming to be unaware that she possessed wings and could have flown up.

I thought of the accidents that might easily happen to a person—or, of course, might not happen, might happen to somebody else. I thought of the dead baby, my sister who might as easily have been I. Would she, then, have been lying here in my place, the sharp grass making its small toothmarks on her brown arms, the sun warming her to the heart? I thought of the leather-bound volumes of Greek, and the six different kinds of iced cakes that used to be offered always in the MacLeod house, and the pictures of leopards and green seas. I thought of my brother, who had been born alive after all, and now had been given his life's name.

I could not really comprehend these things, but I sensed their strangeness, their disarray. I felt that whatever God might love in this world, it was certainly not order.

The Mask of the Bear

In winter my Grandfather Connor used to wear an enormous coat made out of the pelt of a bear. So shaggy and coarse-furred was this coat, so unevenly coloured in patches ranging from amber to near-black, and so vile-smelling when it had become wet with snow, that it seemed to have belonged when it was alive to some lonely and giant Kodiak crankily roaming a high frozen plateau, or an ancient grizzly scarred with battles in the sinister forests of the north. In actuality, it had been an ordinary brown bear and it had come, sad to say, from no more fabled a place than Galloping Mountain, only a hundred miles from Manawaka. The skin had once been given to my grandfather as payment, in the days when he was a blacksmith, before he became a hardware merchant and developed the policy of cash only. He had had it cobbled into a coat by the local shoemaker, and Grandmother Connor had managed to sew in the lining. How long ago that was, no one could say for sure, but my mother, the eldest of his family, said she could not remember a time when he had not worn it. To me, at the age of ten and a half, this meant it must be about a century old. The coat was so heavy that I could not even lift it by myself. I never used to wonder how he could carry that phenomenal weight on himself or why he would choose to, because it was obvious that although he was old he was still an extraordinarily strong man, built to shoulder weights.

Whenever I went into Simlow's Ladies' Wear with

my mother, and made grotesque faces at myself in the long mirror while she tried on dresses, Millie Christopherson who worked there would croon a phrase which made me break into snickering until my mother, who was death on bad manners, tapped anxiously at my shoulders with her slender, nervous hands. *It's you, Mrs. MacLeod*, Millie would say feelingly, *no kidding it's absolutely you.* I appropriated the phrase for my grandfather's winter coat. *It's you,* I would simper nastily at him, although never, of course, aloud.

In my head I sometimes called him "The Great Bear." The name had many associations other than his coat and his surliness. It was the way he would stalk around the Brick House as though it were a cage, on Sundays, impatient for the new week's beginning that would release him into the only freedom he knew, the acts of work. It was the way he would take to the basement whenever a man came to call upon Aunt Edna, which in those days was not often, because—as I had overheard my mother outlining in sighs to my father—most of the single men her age in Manawaka considered that the time she had spent working in Winnipeg had made more difference than it really had, and the situation wasn't helped by her flyaway manner (whatever that might mean). But if ever she was asked out to a movie, and the man was waiting and making stilted weather-chat with Grandmother Connor, Grandfather would prowl through the living room as though seeking a place of rest and not finding it, would stare fixedly without speaking, and would then descend the basement steps to the rocking chair which sat beside the furnace. Above ground, he would not have been found dead sitting in a rocking chair, which he considered a piece of furniture suitable only for the elderly, of whom he was never in his own eyes one. From his cave, however, the angry crunching of the wooden rockers against the cement floor would reverberate throughout the house, a kind of sub-verbal Esperanto, a disapproval which even the most obtuse person could not fail to comprehend.

In some unformulated way, I also associated the secret name with Great Bear Lake, which I had seen only on maps and which I imagined to be a deep vastness of black water, lying somewhere very far beyond our known prairies of tamed fields and barbed-wire fences, somewhere in the regions of jagged rock and eternal ice, where human voices would be drawn into a cold and shadowed stillness without leaving even a trace of warmth.

One Saturday afternoon in January, I was at the rink when my grandfather appeared unexpectedly. He was wearing his formidable coat, and to say he looked out of place among the skaters thronging around the edges of the ice would be putting it mildly. Embarrassed, I whizzed over to him.

"There you are, Vanessa—about time," he said, as though he had been searching for me for hours. "Get your skates off now, and come along. You're to come home with me for supper. You'll be staying the night at our place. Your dad's gone away out to Freehold, and your mother's gone with him. Fine time to pick for it. It's blowing up for a blizzard, if you ask me. They'll not get back for a couple of days, more than likely. Don't see why he don't just tell people to make their own way in to the hospital. Ewen's too easy-going. He'll not get a penny nor a word of thanks for it, you can bet your life on that."

My father and Dr. Cates used to take the country calls in turn. Often when my father went out in the winter, my mother would go with him, in case the old Nash got stuck in the snow and also to talk and thus prevent my father from going to sleep at the wheel, for falling snow has a hypnotic effect.

"What about Roddie?" I asked, for my brother was only a few months old.

"The old lady's keeping care of him," Grandfather Connor replied abruptly.

The old lady meant my Grandmother MacLeod, who was actually a few years younger than Grandfather Connor. He always referred to her in this way, however, as a calculated insult, and here my sympathies were with him for once. He maintained, quite correctly, that she gave herself airs because her husband had been a doctor and now her son was one, and that she looked down on the Connors because they had come from famine Irish (although at least, thank God, Protestant). The two of them seldom met, except at Christmas, and never exchanged more than a few words. If they had ever really clashed it would have been like a brontosaurus running headlong into a tyrannosaurus.

"Hurry along now," he said, when I had taken off my skates and put on my snow boots. "You've got to learn not to dawdle. You're an awful dawdler, Vanessa."

I did not reply. Instead, when we left the rink I began to take exaggeratedly long strides. But he paid no attention to my attempt to reproach him with my speed. He walked beside me steadily and silently, wrapped in his great fur coat and his authority.

The Brick House was at the other end of town, so while I shuffled through the snow and pulled my navy wool scarf up around my nose against the steel cutting edge of the wind, I thought about the story I was setting down in a five-cent scribbler at nights in my room. I was much occupied by the themes of love and death, although my experience of both had so far been gained principally from the Bible, which I read in the same way as I read Eaton's Catalogue or the collected works of Rudyard Kipling—because I had to read something, and the family's finances in the thirties did not permit the purchase of enough volumes of *Doctor Doolittle* or the *Oz* books to keep me going.

For the love scenes, I gained useful material from The Song of Solomon. *Let him kiss me with the kisses of his mouth, for thy love is better than wine,* or *By night on my bed I sought him whom my soul loveth; I sought him but I found him not.* My interpretation was somewhat vague, and I was not helped to any appreciable extent by the explanatory bits in small print at the beginning of each chapter—*The church's love unto Christ. The church's fight and victory in temptation,* et cetera. These explanations did not puzzle me, though, for I assumed even then that they had simply been put there for the benefit of gentle and unworldly people such as my Grandmother Connor, so that they could read the Holy Writ without becoming upset. To me, the woman in The Song was some barbaric queen, beautiful and terrible, and I could imagine her, wearing a long robe of leopard skin and one or two heavy gold bracelets, pacing an alabaster courtyard and keening her unrequited love.

The heroine in my story (which took place in ancient Egypt—my ignorance of this era did not trouble me) was very like the woman in The Song of Solomon, except that mine had long wavy auburn hair, and when her beloved left her, the only thing she could bring herself to eat was an avocado, which seemed to me considerably more stylish and exotic than apples in lieu of love. Her young man was a gifted carver, who had been sent out into the desert by the cruel pharaoh (pharaohs were always cruel—of this I was positive) in order to carve a giant sphinx for the royal tomb. Should I have her die while he was away? Or would it be better if he perished out in the desert? Which of them did I like the least? With the characters whom I liked best, things always turned out right in the end. Yet the death scenes had an undeniable appeal, a sombre splendour, with (as it said in Ecclesiastes) the mourners going about the streets and all the daughters of music brought low. Both death and love seemed regrettably far from Manawaka and the snow, and my grandfather stamping his feet on the front porch of the Brick House and telling me to do the same or I'd be tracking the wet in all over the hardwood floor.

The house was too warm, almost stifling. Grandfather burned mainly birch in the furnace, although it cost twice as much as poplar, and now that he had retired from the hardware store, the furnace gave him something to do and so he was forever stoking it. Grandmother Connor was in the dining room, her stout body in its brown rayon dress bending over the canary's cage.

"Hello, pet," she greeted me. "You should have heard Birdie just a minute ago—one of those real long trills. He's been moulting lately, and this is the first time he's sung in weeks."

"Gee," I said enthusiastically, for although I was not fond of canaries, I was extremely fond of my grandmother. "That's swell. Maybe he'll do it again."

"Messy things, them birds," my grandfather commented. "I can never see what you see in a fool thing like that, Agnes."

My grandmother did not attempt to reply to this. "Would you like a cup of tea, Timothy?" she asked.

"Nearly supper-time, ain't it?"

"Well, not for a little while yet."

"It's away past five," my grandfather said. "What's Edna been doing with herself?"

"She's got the pot-roast in," my grandmother answered, "but it's not done yet."

"You'd think a person could get a meal on time," he said, "considering she's got precious little else to do."

I felt, as so often in the Brick House, that my lungs were in danger of exploding, that the pressure of silence would become too great to be borne. I wanted to point out, as I knew Grandmother Connor would never do, that it wasn't Aunt Edna's fault there were no jobs anywhere these days, and that, as my mother often said of her, she worked her fingers to the bone here so she wouldn't need to feel beholden to him for her keep, and that they would have had to get a hired girl if she hadn't been here, because Grandmother Connor couldn't look after a place this size any more. Also, that the dining-room clock said precisely ten minutes past five, and the evening meal in the Connor house was always at six o'clock on the dot. And—and—a thousand other arguments rose up and nearly choked me. But I did not say anything. I was not that stupid. Instead, I went out to the kitchen.

Aunt Edna was wearing her coral sweater and grey pleated skirt, and I thought she looked lovely, even with her apron on. I always thought she looked lovely, though, whatever she was wearing, but if ever I told her so, she would only laugh and say it was lucky she had a cheering section of one.

"Hello, kiddo," she said. "Do you want to sleep in my room tonight, or shall I make up the bed in the spare room?"

"In your room," I said quickly, for this meant she would let me try out her lipstick and use some of her Jergens hand-lotion, and if I could stay awake until she came to bed, we would whisper after the light was out.

"How's *The Pillars of the Nation* coming along?" she asked.

That had been my epic on pioneer life. I had proceeded to the point in the story where the husband, coming back to the cabin one evening, discovered to his surprise that he was going to become a father. The way he ascertained this interesting fact was that he found his wife constructing a birch-bark cradle. Then came the discovery that Grandfather Connor had been a pioneer, and the story had lost its interest for me. If pioneers were like *that,* I had thought, my pen would be better employed elsewhere.

"I quit that one," I replied laconically. "I'm making up another—it's miles better. It's called *The Silver Sphinx.* I'll bet you can't guess what it's about."

"The desert? Buried treasure? Murder mystery?"

I shook my head.

"Love," I said.

"Good Glory," Aunt Edna said, straight-faced. "That sounds fascinating. Where do you get your ideas, Vanessa?"

I could not bring myself to say the Bible. I was afraid she might think this sounded funny.

"Oh, here and there," I replied noncommittally. "You know."

She gave me an inquisitive glance, as though she meant to question me further, but just then the telephone rang, and I rushed to answer it, thinking it might be my mother or father phoning from Freehold. But it wasn't. It was a voice I didn't know, a man's.

"Is Edna Connor there?"

"Just a minute, please." I cupped one hand over the mouthpiece fixed on the wall, and the other over the receiver.

"For you," I hissed, grinning at her. "A strange man!"

"Mercy," Aunt Edna said ironically, "these hordes of admirers will be the death of me yet. Probably Todd Jeffries from Burns' Electric about that busted lamp."

Nevertheless, she hurried over. Then, as she listened, her face became startled, and something else which I could not fathom.

"Heavens, where are you?" she cried at last. "At the station *here?* Oh Lord. Why didn't you write to say you were—well, sure I am, but—oh, never mind. No, you wait there. I'll come and meet you. You'd never find the house—"

I had never heard her talk this way before, rattlingly. Finally she hung up. Her face looked like a stranger's, and for some reason this hurt me.

"It's Jimmy Lorimer," she said. "He's at the C.P.R. station. He's coming here. Oh my God, I wish Beth were here."

"Why?" I wished my mother were here, too, but I could not see what difference it made to Aunt Edna. I knew who Jimmy Lorimer was. He was a man Aunt Edna had gone around with when she was in Winnipeg. He had given her the Attar of Roses in an atomiser bottle with a green net-covered bulb—the scent she always sprayed around her room after she had had a cigarette there. Jimmy Lorimer had been invested with a remote glamour in my imagination, but all at once I felt I was going to hate him.

I realised that Aunt Edna was referring to what Grandfather Connor might do or say, and instantly I was ashamed for having felt churlishly disposed towards Jimmy Lorimer. Even if he was a cad, a heel, or a nitwit, I swore I would welcome him. I visualised him as having a flashy appearance, like a riverboat gambler in a movie I had seen once, a checkered suit, a slender oiled moustache, a diamond tiepin, a dangerous leer. Never mind. Never mind if he was Lucifer himself.

"I'm glad he's coming," I said staunchly.

Aunt Edna looked at me queerly, her mouth wavering as though she were about to smile. Then, quickly, she bent and hugged me, and I could feel her trembling. At this moment, Grandmother Connor came into the kitchen.

"You all right, pet?" she asked Aunt Edna. "Nothing's the matter, is it?"

"Mother, that was an old friend of mine on the phone just now. Jimmy Lorimer. He's from Winnipeg. He's passing through Manawaka. Is it all right if he comes here for dinner?"

"Well, of course, dear," Grandmother said. "What a lucky thing we're having the pot-roast. There's plenty. Vanessa, pet, you run down to the fruit cellar and bring up a jar of strawberries, will you? Oh, and a small jar of chili sauce. No, maybe the sweet mustard pickle would go better with the pot-roast. What do you think, Edna?"

She spoke as though this were the only important issue in the whole situation. But all the time her eyes were on Aunt Edna's face.

"Edna—" she said, with great effort, "is he—is he a good man, Edna?"

Aunt Edna blinked and looked confused, as though she had been spoken to in some foreign language.

"Yes," she replied.

"You're sure, pet?"

"Yes," Aunt Edna repeated, a little more emphatically than before.

Grandmother Connor nodded, smiled reassuringly, and patted Aunt Edna lightly on the wrist.

"Well, that's fine, dear. I'll just tell Father. Everything will be all right, so don't you worry about a thing."

When Grandmother had gone back to the living room, Aunt Edna began pulling on her black fur-topped overshoes. When she spoke, I didn't know whether it was to me or not.

"I didn't tell her a damn thing," she said in a surprised tone. "I wonder how she knows, or if she really does? *Good.* What a word. I wish I didn't know what she means when she says that. Or else that she knew what I mean when I say it. Glory, I wish Beth were here."

I understood then that she was not speaking to me, and that what she had to say could not be spoken to me. I felt chilled by my childhood, unable to touch her because of the freezing burden of my inexperience. I was about to say something, anything, however mistaken, when my aunt said *Sh*, and we both listened to the talk from the living room.

"A friend of Edna's is coming for dinner, Timothy," Grandmother was saying quietly. "A young man from Winnipeg."

A silence. Then, "Winnipeg!" my grandfather exclaimed, making it sound as though Jimmy Lorimer were coming here straight from his harem in Casablanca.

"What's he do?" Grandfather demanded next.

"Edna didn't say."

"I'm not surprised," Grandfather said darkly. "Well, I won't have her running around with that sort of fellow. She's got no more sense than a sparrow."

"She's twenty-eight," Grandmother said, almost apologetically. "Anyway, this is just a friend."

"Friend!" my grandfather said, annihilating the word. Then, not loudly, but with an odd vehemence, "you don't know a blame thing about men, Agnes. You never have."

Even I could think of several well-placed replies that my grandmother might have made, but she did not do so. She did not say anything. I looked at Aunt Edna, and saw that she had closed her eyes the way people do when they have a headache. Then we heard Grandmother's voice, speaking at last, not in her usual placid and unruffled way, but hesitantly.

"Timothy—please. Be nice to him. For my sake."

For my sake. This was so unlike my grandmother that I was stunned. She was not a person who begged you to be kind for her sake, or even for God's sake. If you were kind, in my grandmother's view, it was for its own sake, and the judgement of whether you had done well or not was up to the Almighty. *Judge not, that ye be not judged*—this was her favourite admonition to me when I lost my temper with one of my friends. As a devout Baptist, she believed it was a sin to pray for anything for yourself. You ought to pray only for strength to bear whatever the Lord saw fit to send you, she thought. I was never able to follow this advice, for although I would often feel a sense of uneasiness over the tone of my prayers, I was the kind of person who prayed frantically—"Please, God, please, please *please* let Ross MacVey like me better than Mavis." Grandmother Connor was not self-effacing in her lack of demands either upon God or upon her family. She merely believed that what happened to a person in this life was in Other Hands. Acceptance was at the heart of her. I don't think in her own eyes she ever lived in a state of bondage. To the rest of the family, thrashing furiously and uselessly in various snarled dilemmas, she must often have appeared to live in a state of perpetual grace, but I am certain she didn't think of it that way, either.

Grandfather Connor did not seem to have heard her.

"We won't get our dinner until all hours, I daresay," he said.

But we got our dinner as soon as Aunt Edna had

arrived back with Jimmy Lorimer, for she flew immediately out to the kitchen and before we knew it we were all sitting at the big circular table in the dining room.

Jimmy Lorimer was not at all what I had expected. Far from looking like a Mississippi gambler, he looked just like anybody else, any uncle or grown-up cousin, unexceptional in every way. He was neither overwhelmingly handsome nor interestingly ugly. He was okay to look at, but as I said to myself, feeling at the same time a twinge of betrayal towards Aunt Edna, he was nothing to write home about. He wore a brown suit and a green tie. The only thing about him which struck fire was that he had a joking manner similar to Aunt Edna's, but whereas I felt at ease with this quality in her, I could never feel comfortable with the laughter of strangers, being uncertain where an including laughter stopped and taunting began.

"You're from Winnipeg, eh?" Grandfather Connor began. "Well, I guess you fellows don't put much store in a town like Manawaka."

Without waiting for affirmation or denial of this sentiment, he continued in an unbroken line.

"I got no patience with these people who think a small town is just nothing. You take a city, now. You could live in one of them places for twenty years, and you'd not get to know your next-door neighbour. Trouble comes along—who's going to give you a hand? Not a blamed soul."

Grandfather Connor had never in his life lived in a city, so his first-hand knowledge of their ways was, to say the least, limited. As for trouble—the thought of my grandfather asking any soul in Manawaka to give aid and support to him in any way whatsoever was inconceivable. He would have died of starvation, physical or spiritual, rather than put himself in any man's debt by so much as a dime or a word.

"Hey, hold on a minute," Jimmy Lorimer protested. "I never said that about small towns. As a mat-

61

ter of fact, I grew up in one myself. I came from McConnell's Landing. Ever heard of it?"

"I heard of it all right," Grandfather said brusquely, and no one could have told from his tone whether McConnell's Landing was a place of ill-repute or whether he simply felt his knowledge of geography was being doubted. "Why'd you leave, then?"

Jimmy shrugged. "Not much opportunity there. Had to seek my fortune, you know. Can't say I've found it, but I'm still looking."

"Oh, you'll be a tycoon yet, no doubt," Aunt Edna put in.

"You bet your life, kiddo," Jimmy replied. "You wait. Times'll change."

I didn't like to hear him say "kiddo." It was Aunt Edna's word, the one she called me by. It didn't belong to him.

"Mercy, they can't change fast enough for me," Aunt Edna said. "I guess I haven't got your optimism, though."

"Well, I haven't got it, either," he said, laughing, "but keep it under your hat, eh?"

Grandfather Connor had listened to this exchange with some impatience. Now he turned to Jimmy once more.

"What's your line of work?"

"I'm with Reliable Loan Company right now, Mr. Connor, but I don't aim to stay there permanently. I'd like to have my own business. Cars are what I'm really interested in. But it's not so easy to start up these days."

Grandfather Connor's normal opinions on social issues possessed such a high degree of clarity and were so frequently stated that they were well known even to me—all labour unions were composed of thugs and crooks; if people were unemployed it was due to their own laziness; if people were broke it was because they were not thrifty. Now, however, a look of intense and brooding sorrow came into his face, as he became all at once the champion of the poor and oppressed.

"Loan company!" he said. "Them blood-suckers. They wouldn't pay no mind to how hard-up a man might be. Take everything he has, without batting an eye. By the Lord Harry, I never thought the day would come when I'd sit down to a meal alongside one of them fellows."

Aunt Edna's face was rigid.

"Jimmy," she said. "Ignore him."

Grandfather turned on her, and they stared at one another with a kind of inexpressible rage but neither of them spoke. I could not help feeling sorry for Jimmy Lorimer, who mumbled something about his train leaving and began eating hurriedly. Grandfather rose to his feet.

"I've had enough," he said.

"Don't you want your dessert, Timothy?" Grandmother asked, as though it never occurred to her that he could be referring to anything other than the meal. It was only then that I realised that this was the first time she had spoken since we sat down at the table. Grandfather did not reply. He went down to the basement. Predictably, in a moment we could hear the wooden rockers of his chair thudding like retreating thunder. After dinner, Grandmother sat in the living room, but she did not get out the red cardigan she was knitting for me. She sat without doing anything, quite still, her hands folded in her lap.

"I'll let you off the dishes tonight, honey," Aunt Edna said to me. "Jimmy will help with them. You can try out my lipstick, if you like, only for Pete's sake wash it off before you come down again."

I went upstairs, but I did not go to Aunt Edna's room. I went into the back bedroom to one of my listening posts. In the floor there was a round hole which had once been used for a stove-pipe leading up from the kitchen. Now it was covered with a piece of brown-painted tin full of small perforations which had apparently been noticed only by me.

"Where does he get his lines, Edna?" Jimmy was saying. "He's like old-time melodrama."

"Yeh, I know." Aunt Edna sounded annoyed. "But let me say it, eh?"

"Sorry. Honest. Listen, can't you even—"

Scuffling sounds, then my aunt's nervous whisper.

"Not here, Jimmy. Please. You don't understand what they're—"

"I understand, all right. Why in God's name do you stay, Edna? Aren't you ever coming back? That's what I want to know."

"With no job? Don't make me laugh."

"I could help out, at first anyway—"

"Jimmy, don't talk like a lunatic. Do you really think I could?"

"Oh hell, I suppose not. Well, look at it this way. What if I wasn't cut out for the unattached life after all? What if the old leopard actually changed his spots, kiddo? What would you say to that?"

A pause, as though Aunt Edna were mulling over his words.

"That'll be the day," she replied. "I'll believe it when I see it."

"Well, Jesus, lady," he said, "I'm not getting down on my knees. Tell me one thing, though—don't you miss me at all? Don't you miss—everything? C'mon now—don't you? Not even a little bit?"

Another pause. She could not seem to make up her mind how to respond to the teasing quality of his voice.

"Yeh, I lie awake nights," she said at last, sarcastically.

He laughed. "Same old Edna. Want me to tell you something, kiddo? I think you're scared."

"Scared?" she said scornfully. "Me? That'll be the fair and frosty Friday."

Although I spent so much of my life listening to conversations which I was not meant to overhear, all at once I felt, for the first time, sickened by what I was doing. I left my listening post and tiptoed into Aunt Edna's room. I wondered if someday I would be the one who was doing the talking, while another child would be doing the listening. This gave me an unpleasantly eerie feeling. I tried on Aunt Edna's lipstick and rouge, but my heart was not in it.

When I went downstairs again, Jimmy Lorimer was just leaving. Aunt Edna went to her room and closed the door. After a while she came out and asked me if I would mind sleeping in the spare bedroom that night after all, so that was what I did.

I woke in the middle of the night. When I sat up, feeling strange because I was not in my own bed at home, I saw through the window a glancing light on the snow. I got up and peered out, and there were the northern lights whirling across the top of the sky like lightning that never descended to earth. The yard of the Brick House looked huge, a white desert, and the pale gashing streaks of light pointed up the caverns and the hollowed places where the wind had sculptured the snow.

I could not stand being alone another second, so I walked in my bare feet along the hall. From Grandfather's room came the sound of grumbling snores, and from Grandmother's room no sound at all. I stopped beside the door of Aunt Edna's room. It seemed to me that she would not mind if I entered quietly, so as not to disturb her, and crawled in beside her. Maybe she would even waken and say, "It's okay, kiddo—your dad phoned after you'd gone to sleep—they got back from Freehold all right."

Then I heard her voice, and the held-in way she was crying, and the name she spoke, as though it hurt her to speak it even in a whisper.

Like some terrified poltergeist, I flitted back to the spare room and whipped into bed. I wanted only to forget that I had heard anything, but I knew I would not forget. There arose in my mind, mysteriously, the picture of a barbaric queen, someone who had lived a long time ago. I could not reconcile this image with the known face, nor could I disconnect it. I thought of my aunt, her sturdy laughter, the way she tore into the housework, her hands and feet which she always disparagingly joked about, believing them to be clumsy. I thought of the story in the scribbler at home. I wanted to get home quickly, so I could destroy it.

Whenever Grandmother Connor was ill, she would not see any doctor except my father. She did not believe in surgery, for she thought it was tampering with the Divine Intention, and she was always afraid that Dr. Cates would operate on her without her consent. She trusted my father implicitly, and when he went into the room where she lay propped up on pillows, she would say, "Here's Ewen—now everything will be fine," which both touched and alarmed my father, who said he hoped she wasn't putting her faith in a broken reed.

Late that winter, she became ill again. She did not go into hospital, so my mother, who had been a nurse, moved down to the Brick House to look after her. My brother and I were left in the adamant care of Grandmother MacLeod. Without my mother, our house seemed like a museum, full of dead and meaningless objects, vases and gilt-framed pictures and looming furniture, all of which had to be dusted and catered to, for reasons which everyone had forgotten. I was not allowed to see Grandmother Connor, but every day after school I went to the Brick House to see my mother. I always asked impatiently, "When is Grandmother going to be better?" and my mother would reply, "I don't know, dear. Soon, I hope." But she did not sound very certain, and I imagined the leaden weeks going by like this, with her away, and Grandmother MacLeod poking her head into my bedroom doorway each morning and telling me to be sure to make my bed because a slovenly room meant a slovenly heart.

But the weeks did not go by like this. One afternoon when I arrived at the Brick House, Grandfather

Connor was standing out on the front porch. I was startled, because he was not wearing his great bear coat. He wore no coat at all, only his dingy serge suit, although the day was fifteen below zero. The blown snow had sifted onto the porch and lay in thin drifts. He stood there by himself, his yellowish-white hair plumed by a wind which he seemed not to notice, his bony and still-handsome face not averted at all from the winter. He looked at me as I plodded up the path and the front steps.

"Vanessa, your grandmother's dead," he said.

Then, as I gazed at him, unable to take in the significance of what he had said, he did a horrifying thing. He gathered me into the relentless grip of his arms. He bent low over me, and sobbed against the cold skin of my face.

I wanted only to get away, to get as far away as possible and never come back. I wanted desperately to see my mother, yet I felt I could not enter the house, not ever again. Then my mother opened the front door and stood there in the doorway, her slight body shivering. Grandfather released me, straightened, became again the carved face I had seen when I approached the house.

"Father," my mother said. "Come into the house. Please."

"In a while, Beth," he replied tonelessly. "Never you mind."

My mother held out her hands to me, and I ran to her. She closed the door and led me into the living room. We both cried, and yet I think I cried mainly because she did, and because I had been shocked by my grandfather. I still could not believe that anyone I cared about could really die.

Aunt Edna came into the living room. She hesitated, looking at my mother and me. Then she turned and went back to the kitchen, stumblingly. My mother's hands made hovering movements and she half rose from the chesterfield, then she held me closely again.

"It's worse for Edna," she said. "I've got you and Roddie, and your dad."

I did not fully realise yet that Grandmother Connor would never move around this house again, preserving its uncertain peace somehow. Yet all at once I knew how it would be for Aunt Edna, without her, alone in the Brick House with Grandfather Connor. I had not known at all that a death would be like this, not only one's own pain, but the almost unbearable knowledge of that other pain which could not be reached nor lessened.

My mother and I went out to the kitchen, and the three of us sat around the oilcloth-covered table, scarcely talking but needing one another at least to be there. We heard the front door open, and Grandfather Connor came back into the house. He did not come out to the kitchen, though. He went, as though instinctively, to his old cavern. We heard him walking heavily down the basement steps.

"Edna—should we ask him if he wants to come and have some tea?" my mother said. "I hate to see him going like that—there—"

Aunt Edna's face hardened.

"I don't want to see him, Beth," she replied, forcing the words out. "I can't. Not yet. All I'd be able to think of is how he was—with her."

"Oh honey, I know," my mother said. "But you mustn't let yourself dwell on that now."

"The night Jimmy was here," my aunt said distinctly, "she asked Father to be nice, for her sake. For her sake, Beth. For the sake of all the years, if they'd meant anything at all. But he couldn't even do that. Not even that."

Then she put her head down on the table and cried in a way I had never heard any person cry before, as though there were no end to it anywhere.

I was not allowed to attend Grandmother Connor's funeral, and for this I was profoundly grateful, for I had dreaded going. The day of the funeral, I stayed alone in the Brick House, waiting for the family to return. My Uncle Terence, who lived in Toronto, was the only one who had come from a distance. Uncle Will lived in Florida, and Aunt Florence was in England, both too far away. Aunt Edna and my mother were always criticising Uncle Terence and also making excuses for him. He drank more than was good for him—this was one of the numerous fractured bones in the family skeleton which I was not supposed to know about. I was fond of him for the same reason I was fond of Grandfather's horse-trader brother, my Great-Uncle Dan—because he had gaiety and was publicly reckoned to be no good.

I sat in the dining room beside the gilt-boned cage that housed the canary. Yesterday, Aunt Edna, cleaning here, had said, "What on earth are we going to do with the canary? Maybe we can find somebody who would like it."

Grandfather Connor had immediately lit into her. "Edna, your mother liked that bird, so it's staying, do you hear?"

When my mother and Aunt Edna went upstairs to have a cigarette, Aunt Edna had said, "Well, it's dandy that he's so set on the bird now, isn't it? He might have considered that a few years earlier, if you ask me."

"Try to be patient with him," my mother had said. "He's feeling it, too."

"I guess so," Aunt Edna had said in a discouraged voice. "I haven't got Mother's patience, that's all. Not with him, nor with any man."

And I had been reminded then of the item I had seen not long before in the Winnipeg *Free Press,* on the social page, telling of the marriage of James Reilly Lorimer to Somebody-or-other. I had rushed to my mother with the paper in my hand, and she had said, "I know, Vanessa. She knows, too. So let's not bring it up, eh?"

The canary, as usual, was not in a vocal mood, and I sat beside the cage dully, not caring, not even trying to prod the creature into song. I wondered if Grandmother Connor was at this very moment in heaven, that dubious place.

"She believed, Edna," my mother had said defensively. "What right have we to say it isn't so?"

"Oh, I know," Aunt Edna had replied. "But can you take it in, really, Beth?"

"No, not really. But you feel, with someone like her—it would be so awful if it didn't happen, after she'd thought like that for so long."

"She wouldn't know," Aunt Edna had pointed out.

"I guess that's what I can't accept," my mother had said slowly. "I still feel she must be somewhere."

I wanted now to hold my own funeral service for my grandmother, in the presence only of the canary. I went to the bookcase where she kept her Bible, and looked up Ecclesiastes. I intended to read the part about the mourners going about the streets, and the silver cord loosed and the golden bowl broken, and the dust returning to the earth as it was and the spirit unto God who gave it. But I got stuck on the first few lines, because is seemed to me, frighteningly, that they were being spoken in my grandmother's mild voice— *Remember now thy Creator in the days of thy youth, while the evil days come not—*

Then, with a burst of opening doors, the family had returned from the funeral. While they were taking off their coats, I slammed the Bible shut and sneaked it back into the bookcase without anyone's having noticed.

Grandfather Connor walked over to me and placed his hands on my shoulders, and I could do nothing except endure his touch.

"Vanessa—" he said gruffly, and I had at the time no idea how much it cost him to speak at all, "she was an angel. You remember that."

Then he went down to the basement by himself. No one attempted to follow him, or to ask him to come and join the rest of us. Even I, in the confusion of my lack of years, realised that this would have been an impossibility. He was, in some way, untouchable. Whatever his grief was, he did not want us to look at it and we did not want to look at it, either.

Uncle Terence went straight into the kitchen, brought out his pocket flask, and poured a hefty slug of whiskey for himself. He did the same for my mother and father and Aunt Edna.

"Oh Glory," Aunt Edna said with a sigh, "do I ever need this. All the same, I feel we shouldn't, right immediately afterwards. You know—considering how she always felt about it. Supposing Father comes up—"

"It's about time you quit thinking that way, Edna," Uncle Terence said.

Aunt Edna felt in her purse for a cigarette. Uncle Terence reached over and lit it for her. Her hands were unsteady.

"You're telling me," she said.

Uncle Terence gave me a quizzical and yet resigned look, and I knew then that my presence was placing a constraint upon them. When my father said he had to go back to the hospital, I used his departure to slip upstairs to my old post, the deserted stove-pipe hole. I could no longer eavesdrop with a clear conscience, but I justified it now by the fact that I had voluntarily removed myself from the kitchen, knowing they would not have told me to run along, not today.

"An angel," Aunt Edna said bitterly. "Did you hear what he said to Vanessa? It's a pity he never said as much to Mother once or twice, isn't it?"

"She knew how much he thought of her," my mother said.

"Did she?" Aunt Edna said. "I don't believe she ever knew he cared about her at all. I don't think I knew it myself, until I saw how her death hit him."

"That's an awful thing to say!" my mother cried. "Of course she knew, Edna."

"How would she know," Aunt Edna persisted, "if he never let on?"

"How do you know he didn't?" my mother countered. "When they were by themselves."

"I don't know, of course," Aunt Edna said. "But I have my damn shrewd suspicions."

"Did you ever know, Beth," Uncle Terence enquired, pouring himself another drink, "that she almost left him once? That was before you were born, Edna."

"No," my mother said incredulously. "Surely not."

"Yeh. Aunt Mattie told me. Apparently Father carried on for a while with some girl in Winnipeg, and Mother found out about it. She never told him she'd considered leaving him. She only told God and Aunt Mattie. The three of them thrashed it out together, I suppose. Too bad she never told him. It would've been a relief to him, no doubt, to see she wasn't all calm forgiveness."

"How could he?" my mother said in a low voice. "Oh Terence. How could he have done that? To Mother, of all people."

"You know something, Beth?" Uncle Terence said. "I think he honestly believed that about her being some kind of angel. She'd never have thought of herself like that, so I don't suppose it ever would have occurred to her that he did. But I have a notion that he felt all along she was far and away too good for him. Can you feature going to bed with an angel, honey? It doesn't bear thinking about."

"Terence, you're drunk," my mother said sharply. "As usual."

"Maybe so," he admitted. Then he burst out, "I only felt, Beth, that somebody might have said to Vanessa just now, *Look, baby, she was terrific and we thought the world of her, but let's not say angel, eh?* All this angel business gets us into really deep water, you know that?"

"I don't see how you can talk like that, Terence," my mother said, trying not to cry. "Now all of a sudden everything was her fault. I just don't see how you can."

"I'm not saying it was her fault," Uncle Terence

said wearily. "That's not what I meant. Give me credit for one or two brains, Beth. I'm only saying it might have been rough for him, as well, that's all. How do any of us know what he's had to carry on his shoulders? Another person's virtues could be an awful weight to tote around. We all loved her. Whoever loved him? Who in hell could? Don't you think he knew that? Maybe he even thought sometimes it was no more than was coming to him."

"Oh—" my mother said bleakly. "That can't be so. That would be—oh, Terence, do you really think he might have thought that way?"

"I don't know any more than you do, Beth. I think he knew quite well that she had something he didn't, but I'd be willing to bet he always imagined it must be righteousness. It wasn't. It was—well, I guess it was tenderness, really. Unfair as you always are about him, Edna, I think you hit the nail on the head about one thing. I don't believe Mother ever realised he might have wanted her tenderness. Why should she? He could never show any of his own. All he could ever come out with was anger. Well, everybody to his own shield in this family. I guess I carry mine in my hip pocket. I don't know what yours is, Beth, but Edna's is more like his than you might think."

"Oh yeh?" Aunt Edna said, her voice suddenly rough. "What is it, then, if I may be so bold as to enquire?"

"Wisecracks, honey," Uncle Terence replied, very gently. "Just wisecracks."

They stopped talking, and all I could hear was my aunt's uneven breathing, with no one saying a word. Then I could hear her blowing her nose.

"Mercy, I must look like the wreck of the Hesperus," she said briskly. "I'll bet I haven't got a speck of powder left on. Never mind. I'll repair the ravages later. What about putting the kettle on, Beth? Maybe I should go down and see if he'll have a cup of tea now."

"Yes," my mother said. "That's a good idea. You do that, Edna."

I heard my aunt's footsteps on the basement stairs as she went down into Grandfather Connor's solitary place.

Many years later, when Manawaka was far away from me, in miles and in time, I saw one day in a museum the Bear Mask of the Haida Indians. It was a weird mask. The features were ugly and yet powerful. The mouth was turned down in an expression of sullen rage. The eyes were empty caverns, revealing nothing. Yet as I looked, they seemed to draw my own eyes towards them, until I imagined I could see somewhere within that darkness a look which I knew, a lurking bewilderment. I remembered then that in the days before it became a museum piece, the mask had concealed a man.

A Bird in the House

The parade would be almost over by now, and I had
not gone. My mother had said in a resigned voice,
"All right, Vanessa, if that's the way you feel," making
me suffer twice as many jabs of guilt as I would have
done if she had lost her temper. She and Grandmother
MacLeod had gone off, my mother pulling the low
box-sleigh with Roddie all dolled up in his new red
snowsuit, just the sort of little kid anyone would want
people to see. I sat on the lowest branch of the birch
tree in our yard, not minding the snowy wind, even
welcoming its punishment. I went over my reasons for
not going, trying to believe they were good and sufficient, but in my heart I felt I was betraying my father.
This was the first time I had stayed away from the
Remembrance Day parade. I wondered if he would
notice that I was not there, standing on the sidewalk
at the corner of River and Main while the parade
passed, and then following to the Court House grounds
where the service was held.

I could see the whole thing in my mind. It was
the same every year. The Manawaka Civic Band always led the way. They had never been able to afford
full uniforms, but they had peaked navy-blue caps and
sky-blue chest ribbons. They were joined on Remembrance Day by the Salvation Army band, whose uniforms seemed too ordinary for a parade, for they were
the same ones the bandsmen wore every Saturday
night when they played "Nearer My God to Thee" at
the foot of River Street. The two bands never managed to practise quite enough together, so they did

not keep in time too well. The Salvation Army band invariably played faster, and afterwards my father would say irritably, "They play those marches just like they do hymns, blast them, as though they wouldn't get to heaven if they didn't hustle up." And my mother, who had great respect for the Salvation Army because of the good work they did, would respond chidingly, "Now, now, Ewen—" I vowed I would never say "Now, now" to my husband or children, not that I ever intended having the latter, for I had been put off by my brother Roderick, who was now two years old with wavy hair, and everyone said what a beautiful child. I was twelve, and no one in their right mind would have said what a beautiful child, for I was big-boned like my Grandfather Connor and had straight lanky black hair like a Blackfoot or Cree.

After the bands would come the veterans. Even thinking of them at this distance, in the white and withdrawn quiet of the birch tree, gave me a sense of painful embarrassment. I might not have minded so much if my father had not been among them. How could he go? How could he not see how they all looked? It must have been a long time since they were soldiers, for they had forgotten how to march in step. They were old—that was the thing. My father was bad enough, being almost forty, but he wasn't a patch on Howard Tully from the drugstore, who was completely grey-haired and also fat, or Stewart MacMurchie, who was bald at the back of his head. They looked to me like imposters, plump or spindly caricatures of past warriors. I almost hated them for walking in that limping column down Main. At the Court House, everyone would sing *Lord God of Hosts, be with us yet, lest we forget, lest we forget.* Will Masterson would pick up his old Army bugle and blow the Last Post. Then it would be over and everyone could start gabbling once more and go home.

I jumped down from the birch bough and ran to the house, yelling, making as much noise as I could.

A Bird in the House

I'm a poor lonesome cowboy
An' a long way from home—

I stepped inside the front hall and kicked off my
snow boots. I slammed the door behind me, making
the dark ruby and emerald glass shake in the small
leaded panes. I slid purposely on the hall rug, causing
it to bunch and crinkle on the slippery polished oak
of the floor. I seized the newel post, round as a head,
and spun myself to and fro on the bottom stair.

I ain't got no father
To buy the clothes I wear.
I'm a poor lonesome—

At this moment my shoulders were firmly seized
and shaken by a pair of hands, white and delicate and
old, but strong as talons.

"Just what do you think you're doing, young lady?"
Grandmother MacLeod enquired, in a voice like frost
on a windowpane, infinitely cold and clearly etched.

I went limp and in a moment she took her hands
away. If you struggled, she would always hold on
longer.

"Gee, I never knew you were home yet."

"I would have thought that on a day like this you
might have shown a little respect and consideration,"
Grandmother MacLeod said, "even if you couldn't
make the effort to get cleaned up enough to go to the
parade."

I realised with surprise that she imagined this to
be my reason for not going. I did not try to correct her
impression. My real reason would have been even less
acceptable.

"I'm sorry," I said quickly.

In some families, *please* is described as the magic
word. In our house, however, it was *sorry*.

"This isn't an easy day for any of us," she said.

Her younger son, my Uncle Roderick, had been

77

killed in the Great War. When my father marched, and when the hymn was sung, and when that unbearably lonely tune was sounded by the one bugle and everyone forced themselves to keep absolutely still, it would be that boy of whom she was thinking. I felt the enormity of my own offence.

"Grandmother—I'm sorry."

"So you said."

I could not tell her I had not really said it before at all. I went into the den and found my father there. He was sitting in the leather-cushioned armchair beside the fireplace. He was not doing anything, just sitting and smoking. I stood beside him, wanting to touch the light-brown hairs on his forearm, but thinking he might laugh at me or pull his arm away if I did.

"I'm sorry," I said, meaning it.

"What for, honey?"

"For not going."

"Oh—that. What was the matter?"

I did not want him to know, and yet I had to tell him, make him see.

"They look silly," I blurted. "Marching like that."

For a minute I thought he was going to be angry. It would have been a relief to me if he had been. Instead, he drew his eyes away from mine and fixed them above the mantelpiece where the sword hung, the handsome and evil-looking crescent in its carved bronze sheath that some ancestor had once brought from the Northern Frontier of India.

"Is that the way it looks to you?" he said.

I felt in his voice some hurt, something that was my fault. I wanted to make everything all right between us, to convince him that I understood, even if I did not. I prayed that Grandmother MacLeod would stay put in her room, and that my mother would take a long time in the kitchen, giving Roddie his lunch. I wanted my father to myself, so I could prove to him that I cared more about him than any of the others did. I wanted to speak in some way that would be more poignant and comprehending than anything of which my mother could possibly be capable. But I did not know how.

"You were right there when Uncle Roderick got killed, weren't you?" I began uncertainly.

"Yes."

"How old was he, Dad?"

"Eighteen," my father said.

Unexpectedly, that day came into intense being for me. He had had to watch his own brother die, not in the antiseptic calm of some hospital, but out in the open, the stretches of mud I had seen in his snapshots. He would not have known what to do. He would just have had to stand there and look at it, whatever that might mean. I looked at my father with a kind of horrified awe, and then I began to cry. I had forgotten about impressing him with my perception. Now I needed him to console me for this unwanted glimpse of the pain he had once known.

"Hey, cut it out, honey," he said, embarrassed. "It was bad, but it wasn't all as bad as that part. There were a few other things."

"Like what?" I said, not believing him.

"Oh—I don't know," he replied evasively. "Most of us were pretty young, you know, I and the boys I joined up with. None of us had ever been away from Manawaka before. Those of us who came back mostly came back here, or else went no further away from town than Winnipeg. So when we were overseas—that was the only time most of us were ever a long way from home."

"Did you want to be?" I asked, shocked.

"Oh well—" my father said uncomfortably. "It was kind of interesting to see a few other places for a change, that's all."

Grandmother MacLeod was standing in the doorway.

"Beth's called you twice for lunch, Ewen. Are you deaf, you and Vanessa?"

"Sorry," my father and I said simultaneously.

Then we went upstairs to wash our hands.

That winter my mother returned to her old job as nurse in my father's medical practice. She was able to do this only because of Noreen.

"Grandmother MacLeod says we're getting a maid," I said to my father, accusingly, one morning. "We're not, are we?"

"Believe you me, on what I'm going to be paying her," my father growled, "she couldn't be called anything as classy as a maid. Hired girl would be more like it."

"Now, now, Ewen," my mother put in, "it's not as if we were cheating her or anything. You know she wants to live in town, and I can certainly see why, stuck out there on the farm, and her father hardly ever letting her come in. What kind of life is that for a girl?"

"I don't like the idea of your going back to work, Beth," my father said. "I know you're fine now, but you're not exactly the robust type."

"You can't afford to hire a nurse any longer. It's all very well to say the Depression won't last forever—probably it won't, but what else can we do for now?"

"I'm damned if I know," my father admitted. "Beth—"

"Yes?"

They both seemed to have forgotten about me. It was at breakfast, which we always ate in the kitchen, and I sat rigidly on my chair, pretending to ignore and thus snub their withdrawal from me. I glared at the window, but it was so thickly plumed and scrolled with frost that I could not see out. I glanced back to my parents. My father had not replied, and my mother was looking at him in that anxious and half-frowning way she had recently developed.

"What is it, Ewen?" Her voice had the same nervous sharpness it bore sometimes when she would say to me, "For mercy's sake, Vanessa, what is it *now?*" as though whatever was the matter, it was bound to be the last straw.

My father spun his sterling silver serviette ring, engraved with his initials, slowly around on the table.

"I never thought things would turn out like this, did you?"

"Please—" my mother said in a low strained voice, "please, Ewen, let's not start all this again. I can't take it."

"All right," my father said. "Only—"

"The MacLeods used to have money and now they don't," my mother cried. "Well, they're not alone. Do you think all that matters to me, Ewen? What I can't bear is to see you forever reproaching yourself. As if it were your fault."

"I don't think it's the comedown," my father said. "If I were somewhere else, I don't suppose it would matter to me, either, except where you're concerned. But I suppose you'd work too hard wherever you were —it's bred into you. If you haven't got anything to slave away at, you'll sure as hell invent something."

"What do you think I should do, let the house go to wrack and ruin? That would go over well with your mother, wouldn't it?"

"That's just it," my father said. "It's the damned house all the time. I haven't only taken on my father's house, I've taken on everything that goes with it, apparently. Sometimes I really wonder—"

"Well, it's a good thing I've inherited some practicality even if you haven't," my mother said. "I'll say that for the Connors—they aren't given to brooding, thank the Lord. Do you want your egg poached or scrambled?"

"Scrambled," my father said. "All I hope is that this Noreen doesn't get married straightaway, that's all."

"She won't," my mother said. "Who's she going to meet who could afford to marry?"

"I marvel at you, Beth," my father said. "You look as though a puff of wind would blow you away. But underneath, by God, you're all hardwood."

"Don't talk stupidly," my mother said. "All I hope is that she won't object to taking your mother's breakfast up on a tray."

"That's right," my father said angrily. "Rub it in."

"Oh Ewen, I'm sorry!" my mother cried, her face suddenly stricken. "I don't know why I say these things. I didn't mean to."

"I know," my father said. "Here, cut it out, honey. Just for God's sake please don't cry."

"I'm sorry," my mother repeated, blowing her nose.

"We're both sorry," my father said. "Not that that changes anything."

After my father had gone, I got down from my chair and went to my mother.

"I don't want you to go back to the office. I don't want a hired girl here. I'll hate her."

My mother sighed, making me feel that I was placing an intolerable burden on her, and yet making me resent having to feel this weight. She looked tired, as she often did these days. Her tiredness bored me, made me want to attack her for it.

"Catch me getting along with a dumb old hired girl," I threatened.

"Do what you like," my mother said abruptly. "What can I do about it?"

And then, of course, I felt bereft, not knowing which way to turn.

My father need not have worried about Noreen getting married. She was, as it turned out, interested not in boys but in God. My mother was relieved about the boys but alarmed about God.

"It isn't natural," she said, "for a girl of seventeen. Do you think she's all right mentally, Ewen?"

When my parents, along with Grandmother Mac-Leod, went to the United Church every Sunday, I was made to go to Sunday school in the church basement, where there were small red chairs which humiliatingly resembled kindergarten furniture, and pictures of Jesus wearing a white sheet and surrounded by a whole lot of well-dressed kids whose mothers obviously had not suffered them to come unto Him until every face and ear was properly scrubbed. Our religious observances also included grace at meals, when my father would mumble "For what we are about to receive the Lord make us truly thankful Amen," running the words together as though they were one long word. My mother approved of these rituals, which seemed decent and moderate to her. Noreen's religion, however, was a different matter. Noreen belonged to the Tabernacle of the Risen and Reborn, and she had got up to testify no less than seven times in the past two years, she told us. My mother, who could not imagine anyone's voluntarily making a public spectacle of themselves, was profoundly shocked by this revelation.

"Don't worry," my father soothed her. "She's all right. She's just had kind of a dull life, that's all."

My mother shrugged and went on worrying and trying to help Noreen without hurting her feelings, by tactful remarks about the advisability of modulating one's voice when singing hymns, and the fact that there was plenty of hot water so Noreen really didn't need to hesitate about taking a bath. She even bought a razor and a packet of blades and whispered to Noreen that any girl who wore transparent blouses so much would probably like to shave under her arms. None of these suggestions had the slightest effect on Noreen. She did not cease belting out hymns at the top of her voice, she bathed once a fortnight, and the sorrel-coloured hair continued to bloom like a thicket of Indian paintbrush in her armpits.

Grandmother MacLeod refused to speak to Noreen. This caused Noreen a certain amount of bewilderment until she finally hit on an answer.

"Your poor grandma," she said. "She is deaf as a post. These things are sent to try us here on earth, Vanessa. But if she makes it into Heaven, I'll bet you anything she will hear clear as a bell."

Noreen and I talked about Heaven quite a lot, and also Hell. Noreen had an intimate and detailed knowledge of both places. She not only knew what they looked like—she even knew how big they were. Heaven was seventy-seven thousand miles square and it had four gates, each one made out of a different kind of precious jewel. The Pearl Gate, the Topaz gate, the Amethyst Gate, the Ruby Gate—Noreen would reel them off, all the gates of Heaven. I told Noreen they sounded like poetry, but she was puzzled by my reaction and said I shouldn't talk that way. If you said poetry, it sounded like it was just made up and not really so, Noreen said.

Hell was larger than Heaven, and when I asked why, thinking of it as something of a comedown for God, Noreen said naturally it had to be bigger because there were a darn sight more people there than in Heaven. Hell was one hundred and ninety million miles deep and was in perpetual darkness, like a cave or under the sea. Even the flames (this was the awful thing) *did not give off any light.*

I did not actually believe in Noreen's doctrines, but the images which they conjured up began to inhabit my imagination. Noreen's fund of exotic knowledge was not limited to religion, although in a way it all seemed related. She could do many things which had a spooky tinge to them. Once when she was making a cake, she found we had run out of eggs. She went outside and gathered a bowl of fresh snow and used it instead. The cake rose like a charm, and I stared at Noreen as though she were a sorceress. In fact, I began to think of her as a sorceress, someone not quite of this earth. There was nothing unearthly about her broad shoulders and hips and her forest of dark red hair, but even these features took on a slightly sinister significance to me. I no longer saw her through the eyes or the expressed opinions of my mother and father, as a girl who had quit school at grade eight and whose life on the farm had been endlessly drab. I knew the truth—Noreen's life had not been drab at all, for she dwelt in a world of violent splendours, a world filled with angels whose wings of delicate light bore real feathers, and saints shining like the dawn, and prophets who spoke in ancient tongues, and the ecstatic souls of the saved, as well as denizens of the lower regions—mean-eyed imps and crooked cloven-hoofed monsters and beasts with the bodies of swine and the human heads of murderers, and lovely depraved jezebels torn by dogs through all eternity. The middle layer of Creation, our earth, was equally full of grotesque presences, for Noreen believed strongly in the visitation of ghosts and the communication with spirits. She could prove this with her Ouija board. We would both place our fingers lightly on the indicator, and it would skim across the board and spell out answers to our questions. I did not believe whole-heartedly in the Ouija board, either, but I was cautious about the kind of question I asked, in case the answer would turn out unfavourable and I would be unable to forget it.

One day Noreen told me she could also make a table talk. We used the small table in my bedroom, and sure enough, it lifted very slightly under our fingertips and tapped once for *Yes*, twice for *No*. Noreen asked if her Aunt Ruthie would get better from the kidney operation, and the table replied *No*. I withdrew my hands.

"I don't want to do it any more."

"Gee, what's the matter, Vanessa?" Noreen's plain placid face creased in a frown. "We only just begun."

"I have to do my homework."

My heart lurched as I said this. I was certain Noreen would know I was lying, and that she would know not by any ordinary perception, either. But her attention had been caught by something else, and I was thankful, at least until I saw what it was.

My bedroom window was not opened in the coldest weather. The storm window, which was fitted outside as an extra wall against the winter, had three small circular holes in its frame so that some fresh air could seep into the house. The sparrow must have been floundering in the new snow on the roof, for it had crawled in through one of these holes and was now caught between the two layers of glass. I could not bear the panic of the trapped bird, and before I realised what I was doing, I had thrown open the bedroom window. I was not releasing the sparrow into any better a situation, I soon saw, for instead of remaining quiet and allowing us to catch it in order to free it, it began flying blindly around the room, hitting the lampshade, brushing against the walls, its wings seeming to spin faster and faster.

I was petrified. I thought I would pass out if those palpitating wings touched me. There was something in the bird's senseless movements that revolted me. I also thought it was going to damage itself, break one of those thin wing-bones, perhaps, and then it would be lying on the floor, dying, like the pimpled and horribly featherless baby birds we saw sometimes on the sidewalks in the spring when they had fallen out of their nests. I was not any longer worried about the sparrow. I wanted only to avoid the sight of it lying broken on the floor. Viciously, I thought that if Noreen said, *God sees the little sparrow fall,* I would kick her in the shins. She did not, however, say this.

"A bird in the house means a death in the house," Noreen remarked.

Shaken, I pulled my glance away from the whirling wings and looked at Noreen.

"What?"

"That's what I've heard said, anyhow."

The sparrow had exhausted itself. It lay on the floor, spent and trembling. I could not bring myself to touch it. Noreen bent and picked it up. She cradled it with great gentleness between her cupped hands. Then we took it downstairs, and when I had opened the back door, Noreen set the bird free.

"Poor little scrap," she said, and I felt struck to the heart, knowing she had been concerned all along about the sparrow, while I, perfidiously, in the chaos of the moment, had been concerned only about myself.

"Wanna do some with the Ouija board, Vanessa?" Noreen asked.

I shivered a little, perhaps only because of the blast of cold air which had come into the kitchen when the door was opened.

"No thanks, Noreen. Like I said, I got my homework to do. But thanks all the same."

"That's okay," Noreen said in her guileless voice. "Any time."

But whenever she mentioned the Ouija board or the talking table, after that, I always found some excuse not to consult these oracles.

"Do you want to come to church with me this evening, Vanessa?" my father asked.

"How come you're going to the evening service?" I enquired.

"Well, we didn't go this morning. We went snowshoeing instead, remember? I think your grandmother was a little bit put out about it. She went alone this morning. I guess it wouldn't hurt you and me, to go now."

We walked through the dark, along the white streets, the snow squeaking dryly under our feet. The streetlights were placed at long intervals along the sidewalks, and around each pole the circle of flimsy light created glistening points of blue and crystal on the crusted snow. I would have liked to take my father's hand, as I used to do, but I was too old for that now. I walked beside him, taking long steps so he would not have to walk more slowly on my account.

The sermon bored me, and I began leafing through the Hymnary for entertainment. I must have drowsed, for the next thing I knew, my father was prodding me and we were on our feet for the closing hymn.

> *Near the Cross, near the Cross,*
> *Be my glory ever,*
> *Till my ransomed soul shall find*
> *Rest beyond the river.*

I knew the tune well, so I sang loudly for the first verse. But the music to that hymn is sombre, and all at once the words themselves seemed too dreadful to be sung. I stopped singing, my throat knotted. I thought I was going to cry, but I did not know why, except that the song recalled to me my Grandmother Connor, who had been dead only a year now. I wondered why her soul needed to be ransomed. If God did not think she was good enough just as she was, then I did not have much use for His opinion. *Rest beyond the river*—was that what had happened to her? She had believed in Heaven, but I did not think that rest beyond the river was quite what she had in mind. To think of her in Noreen's flashy Heaven, though—that was even worse. Someplace where nobody ever got annoyed or had to be smoothed down and placated, someplace where there were never any family scenes—that would have suited my Grandmother Connor. Maybe she wouldn't have minded a certain amount of rest beyond the river, at that.

When we had the silent prayer, I looked at my father. He sat with his head bowed and his eyes closed. He was frowning deeply, and I could see the pulse in his temple. I wondered then what he believed. I did not have any real idea what it might be. When he raised his head, he did not look uplifted or anything like that. He merely looked tired. Then Reverend McKee pronounced the benediction, and we could go home.

"What do you think about all that stuff, Dad?" I asked hesitantly, as we walked.

"What stuff, honey?"

"Oh, Heaven and Hell, and like that."

My father laughed. "Have you been listening to Noreen too much? Well, I don't know. I don't think they're actual places. Maybe they stand for something that happens all the time here, or else doesn't happen. It's kind of hard to explain. I guess I'm not so good at explanations."

Nothing seemed to have been made any clearer to me. I reached out and took his hand, not caring that he might think this a babyish gesture.

"I hate that hymn!"

"Good Lord," my father said in astonishment. "Why, Vanessa?"

But I did not know and so could not tell him.

Many people in Manawaka had flu that winter, so my father and Dr. Cates were kept extremely busy. I had flu myself, and spent a week in bed, vomiting only the first day and after that enjoying poor health, as my mother put it, with Noreen bringing me ginger ale and orange juice, and each evening my father putting a wooden tongue-depressor into my mouth and peering down my throat, then smiling and saying he thought I might live after all.

Then my father got sick himself, and had to stay at home and go to bed. This was such an unusual occurrence that it amused me.

"Doctors shouldn't get sick," I told him.

"You're right," he said. "That was pretty bad management."

"Run along now, dear," my mother said.

That night I woke and heard voices in the upstairs hall. When I went out, I found my mother and Grandmother MacLeod, both in their dressing-gowns. With them was Dr. Cates. I did not go immediately to my mother, as I would have done only a year before. I stood in the doorway of my room, squinting against the sudden light.

"Mother—what is it?"

She turned, and momentarily I saw the look on her face before she erased it and put on a contrived calm.

"It's all right," she said. "Dr. Cates has just come to have a look at Daddy. You go on back to sleep."

The wind was high that night, and I lay and

listened to it rattling the storm windows and making the dry and winter-stiffened vines of the Virginia creeper scratch like small persistent claws against the red brick. In the morning, my mother told me that my father had developed pneumonia.

Dr. Cates did not think it would be safe to move my father to the hospital. My mother began sleeping in the spare bedroom, and after she had been there for a few nights, I asked if I could sleep in there too. I thought she would be bound to ask me why, and I did not know what I would say, but she did not ask. She nodded, and in some way her easy agreement upset me.

That night Dr. Cates came again, bringing with him one of the nurses from the hospital. My mother stayed upstairs with them. I sat with Grandmother MacLeod in the living room. That was the last place in the world I wanted to be, but I thought she would be offended if I went off. She sat as straight and rigid as a totem pole and embroidered away at the needle-point cushion cover she was doing. I perched on the edge of the chesterfield and kept my eyes fixed on *The White Company* by Conan Doyle, and from time to time I turned a page. I had already read it three times before, but luckily Grandmother MacLeod did not know that. At nine o'clock she looked at her gold brooch watch, which she always wore pinned to her dress, and told me to go to bed, so I did that.

I wakened in darkness. At first, it seemed to me that I was in my own bed, and everything was as usual, with my parents in their room, and Roddie curled up in the crib in his room, and Grandmother MacLeod sleeping with her mouth open in her enormous spool bed, surrounded by half a dozen framed photos of Uncle Roderick and only one of my father, and Noreen snoring fitfully in the room next to mine, with the dark flames of her hair spreading out across the pillow, and the pink and silver motto cards from the Tabernacle stuck with adhesive tape onto the wall beside her bed—*Lean on Him, Emmanuel Is My Refuge, Rock of Ages Cleft for Me.*

Then in the total night around me, I heard a sound. It was my mother, and she was crying, not loudly at all, but from somewhere very deep inside her. I sat up in bed. Everything seemed to have stopped, not only time but my own heart and blood as well. Then my mother noticed that I was awake.

I did not ask her, and she did not tell me anything. There was no need. She held me in her arms, or I held her, I am not certain which. And after a while the first mourning stopped, too, as everything does sooner or later, for when the limits of endurance have been reached, then people must sleep.

In the days following my father's death, I stayed close beside my mother, and this was only partly for my own consoling. I also had the feeling that she needed my protection. I did not know from what, nor what I could possibly do, but something held me there. Reverend McKee called, and I sat with my grandmother and my mother in the living room. My mother told me I did not need to stay unless I wanted to, but I refused to go. What I thought chiefly was that he would speak of the healing power of prayer, and all that, and it would be bound to make my mother cry again. And in fact, it happened in just that way, but when it actually came, I could not protect her from this assault. I could only sit there and pray my own prayer, which was that he would go away quickly.

My mother tried not to cry unless she was alone or with me. I also tried, but neither of us was entirely successful. Grandmother MacLeod, on the other hand, was never seen crying, not even the day of my father's funeral. But that day, when we had returned to the house and she had taken off her black velvet overshoes and her heavy sealskin coat with its black fur that was the softest thing I had ever touched, she stood in the hallway and for the first time she looked unsteady. When I reached out instinctively towards her, she sighed.

"That's right," she said. "You might just take my arm while I go upstairs, Vanessa."

That was the most my Grandmother MacLeod ever gave in, to anyone's sight. I left her in her bedroom, sitting on the straight chair beside her bed and looking at the picture of my father that had been taken when he graduated from medical college. Maybe she was sorry now that she had only the one photograph of him, but whatever she felt, she did not say.

I went down into the kitchen. I had scarcely spoken to Noreen since my father's death. This had not been done on purpose. I simply had not seen her. I had not really seen anyone except my mother. Looking at Noreen now, I suddenly recalled the sparrow. I felt physically sick, remembering the fearful darting and plunging of those wings, and the fact that it was I who had opened the window and let it in. Then an inexplicable fury took hold of me, some terrifying need to hurt, burn, destroy. Absolutely without warning, either to her or to myself, I hit Noreen as hard as I could. When she swung around, appalled, I hit out at her once more, my arms and legs flailing. Her hands snatched at my wrists, and she held me, but still I continued to struggle, fighting blindly, my eyes tightly closed, as though she were a prison all around me and I was battling to get out. Finally, too shocked at myself to go on, I went limp in her grasp and she let me drop to the floor.

"Vanessa! I never done one single solitary thing to you, and here you go hitting and scratching me like that! What in the world has got into you?"

I began to say I was sorry, which was certainly true, but I did not say it. I could not say anything.

"You're not yourself, what with your dad and everything," she excused me. "I been praying every night that your dad is with God, Vanessa. I know he wasn't actually saved in the regular way, but still and all—"

"Shut up," I said.

Something in my voice made her stop talking. I rose from the floor and stood in the kitchen doorway.

"He didn't need to be saved," I went on coldly, distinctly. "And he is not in Heaven, because there is no Heaven. And it doesn't matter, see? *It doesn't matter!*"

Noreen's face looked peculiarly vulnerable now, her high wide cheekbones and puzzled childish eyes, and the thick russet tangle of her hair. I had not hurt her much before, when I hit her. But I had hurt her now, hurt her in some inexcusable way. Yet I sensed, too, that already she was gaining some satisfaction out of feeling sorrowful about my disbelief.

I went upstairs to my room. Momentarily I felt a sense of calm, almost of acceptance. *Rest beyond the river.* I knew now what that meant. It meant Nothing. It meant only silence, forever.

Then I lay down on my bed and spent the last of my tears, or what seemed then to be the last. Because, despite what I had said to Noreen, it did matter. It mattered, but there was no help for it.

Everything changed after my father's death. The MacLeod house could not be kept up any longer. My mother sold it to a local merchant who subsequently covered the deep red of the brick over with yellow stucco. Something about the house had always made me uneasy—that tower room where Grandmother MacLeod's potted plants drooped in a lethargic and lime-green confusion, those long stairways and hidden places, the attic which I had always imagined to be dwelt in by the spirits of the family dead, that gigantic portrait of the Duke of Wellington at the top of the stairs. It was never an endearing house. And yet when it was no longer ours, and when the Virginia creeper had been torn down and the dark walls turned to a light marigold, I went out of my way to avoid walking past, for it seemed to me that the house had lost the stern dignity that was its very heart.

Noreen went back to the farm. My mother and brother and myself moved into Grandfather Connor's house. Grandmother MacLeod went to live with Aunt Morag in Winnipeg. It was harder for her than for anyone, because so much of her life was bound up with the MacLeod house. She was fond of Aunt Morag, but that hardly counted. Her men were gone, her husband and her sons, and a family whose men are gone is no family at all. The day she left, my mother and I did not know what to say. Grandmother Mac-Leod looked even smaller than usual in her fur coat and her black velvet toque. She became extremely agitated about trivialities, and fussed about the possibility of the taxi not arriving on time. She had forbidden us to accompany her to the station. About my father, or the house, or anything important, she did not say a word. Then, when the taxi had finally arrived, she turned to my mother.

"Roddie will have Ewen's seal ring, of course, with the MacLeod crest on it," she said. "But there is another seal as well, don't forget, the larger one with the crest and motto. It's meant to be worn on a watch chain. I keep it in my jewel-box. It was Roderick's. Roddie's to have that, too, when I die. Don't let Morag talk you out of it."

During the Second World War, when I was seventeen and in love with an airman who did not love me, and desperately anxious to get away from Manawaka and from my grandfather's house, I happened one day to be going through the old mahogany desk that had belonged to my father. It had a number of small drawers inside, and I accidentally pulled one of these all the way out. Behind it there was another drawer, one I had not known about. Curiously, I opened it. Inside there was a letter written on almost transparent paper in a cramped angular handwriting.

It began—*Cher Monsieur Ewen*—That was all I could make out, for the writing was nearly impossible to read and my French was not good. It was dated 1919. With it, there was a picture of a girl, looking absurdly old-fashioned to my eyes, like the faces on long-discarded calendars or chocolate boxes. But beneath the dated quality of the photograph, she seemed neither expensive nor cheap. She looked like what she probably had been—an ordinary middle-class girl, but in another country. She wore her hair in long ringlets, and her mouth was shaped into a sweetly sad posed smile like Mary Pickford's. That was all. There was nothing else in the drawer.

I looked for a long time at the girl, and hoped she had meant some momentary and unexpected freedom. I remembered what he had said to me, after I hadn't gone to the Remembrance Day parade.

"What are you doing, Vanessa?" my mother called from the kitchen.

"Nothing," I replied.

I took the letter and picture outside and burned them. That was all I could do for him. Now that we might have talked together, it was many years too late. Perhaps it would not have been possible anyway. I did not know.

As I watched the smile of the girl turn into scorched paper, I grieved for my father as though he had just died now.

The Loons

Just below Manawaka, where the Wachakwa River
ran brown and noisy over the pebbles, the scrub oak
and grey-green willow and chokecherry bushes grew
in a dense thicket. In a clearing at the centre of
the thicket stood the Tonnerre family's shack. The
basis of this dwelling was a small square cabin made
of poplar poles and chinked with mud, which had
been built by Jules Tonnerre some fifty years before,
when he came back from Batoche with a bullet in his
thigh, the year that Riel was hung and the voices of the
Metis entered their long silence. Jules had only intended to stay the winter in the Wachakwa Valley,
but the family was still there in the thirties, when I
was a child. As the Tonnerres had increased, their
settlement had been added to, until the clearing at
the foot of the town hill was a chaos of lean-tos, wood-
en packing cases, warped lumber, discarded car tires,
ramshackle chicken coops, tangled strands of barbed
wire and rusty tin cans.

The Tonnerres were French halfbreeds, and
among themselves they spoke a *patois* that was neither Cree nor French. Their English was broken and
full of obscenities. They did not belong among the
Cree of the Galloping Mountain reservation, further
north, and they did not belong among the Scots-Irish
and Ukrainians of Manawaka, either. They were, as
my Grandmother MacLeod would have put it, neither
flesh, fowl, nor good salt herring. When their men were
not working at odd jobs or as section hands on the
C.P.R., they lived on relief. In the summers, one of

the Tonnerre youngsters, with a face that seemed totally unfamiliar with laughter, would knock at the doors of the town's brick houses and offer for sale a lard-pail full of bruised wild strawberries, and if he got as much as a quarter he would grab the coin and run before the customer had time to change her mind. Sometimes old Jules, or his son Lazarus, would get mixed up in a Saturday-night brawl, and would hit out at whoever was nearest, or howl drunkenly among the offended shoppers on Main Street, and then the Mountie would put them for the night in the barred cell underneath the Court House, and the next morning they would be quiet again.

Piquette Tonnerre, the daughter of Lazarus, was in my class at school. She was older than I, but she had failed several grades, perhaps because her attendance had always been sporadic and her interest in school-work negligible. Part of the reason she had missed a lot of school was that she had had tuberculosis of the bone, and had once spent many months in hospital. I knew this because my father was the doctor who had looked after her. Her sickness was almost the only thing I knew about her, however. Otherwise, she existed for me only as a vaguely embarrassing presence, with her hoarse voice and her clumsy limping walk and her grimy cotton dresses that were always miles too long. I was neither friendly nor unfriendly towards her. She dwelt and moved somewhere within my scope of vision, but I did not actually notice her very much until that peculiar summer when I was eleven.

"I don't know what to do about that kid," my father said at dinner one evening. "Piquette Tonnerre, I mean. The damn bone's flared up again. I've had her in hospital for quite a while now, and it's under control all right, but I hate like the dickens to send her home again."

"Couldn't you explain to her mother that she has to rest a lot?" my mother said.

"The mother's not there," my father replied. "She

took off a few years back. Can't say I blame her.
Piquette cooks for them, and she says Lazarus would
never do anything for himself as long as she's there.
Anyway, I don't think she'd take much care of herself,
once she got back. She's only thirteen, after all. Beth, I
was thinking—what about taking her up to Diamond
Lake with us this summer? A couple of months rest
would give that bone a much better chance."

My mother looked stunned.

"But Ewen—what about Roddie and Vanessa?"

"She's not contagious," my father said. "And it
would be company for Vanessa."

"Oh dear," my mother said in distress, "I'll bet
anything she has nits in her hair."

"For Pete's sake," my father said crossly, "do you
think Matron would let her stay in the hospital for all
this time like that? Don't be silly, Beth."

Grandmother MacLeod, her delicately featured
face as rigid as a cameo, now brought her mauve-
veined hands together as though she were about to
begin a prayer.

"Ewen, if that half-breed youngster comes along
to Diamond Lake, I'm not going," she announced. "I'll
go to Morag's for the summer."

I had trouble in stifling my urge to laugh, for my
mother brightened visibly and quickly tried to hide it.
If it came to a choice between Grandmother Mac-
Leod and Piquette, Piquette would win hands down,
nits or not.

"It might be quite nice for you, at that," she
mused. "You haven't seen Morag for over a year, and
you might enjoy being in the city for a while. Well,
Ewen dear, you do what you think best. If you think it
would do Piquette some good, then we'll be glad to
have her, as long as she behaves herself."

So it happened that several weeks later, when we
all piled into my father's old Nash, surrounded by
suitcases and boxes of provisions and toys for my ten-
month-old brother, Piquette was with us and Grandmother MacLeod, miraculously, was not. My father

would only be staying at the cottage for a couple of weeks, for he had to get back to his practice, but the rest of us would stay at Diamond Lake until the end of August.

Our cottage was not named, as many were, "Dew Drop Inn" or "Bide-a-Wee," or "Bonnie Doon." The sign on the roadway bore in austere letters only our name, MacLeod. It was not a large cottage, but it was on the lakefront. You could look out the windows and see, through the filigree of the spruce trees, the water glistening greenly as the sun caught it. All around the cottage were ferns, and sharp-branched raspberry bushes, and moss that had grown over fallen tree trunks. If you looked carefully among the weeds and grass, you could find wild strawberry plants which were in white flower now and in another month would bear fruit, the fragrant globes hanging like miniature scarlet lanterns on the thin hairy stems. The two grey squirrels were still there, gossiping at us from the tall spruce beside the cottage, and by the end of the summer they would again be tame enough to take pieces of crust from my hands. The broad moose antlers that hung above the back door were a little more bleached and fissured after the winter, but otherwise everything was the same. I raced joyfully around my kingdom, greeting all the places I had not seen for a year. My brother, Roderick, who had not been born when we were here last summer, sat on the car rug in the sunshine and examined a brown spruce cone, meticulously turning it round and round in his small and curious hands. My mother and father toted the luggage from car to cottage, exclaiming over how well the place had wintered, no broken windows, thank goodness, no apparent damage from storm-felled branches or snow.

Only after I had finished looking around did I notice Piquette. She was sitting on the swing, her lame leg held stiffly out, and her other foot scuffing the ground as she swung slowly back and forth. Her long hair hung black and straight around her shoulders, and

her broad coarse-featured face bore no expression—
it was blank, as though she no longer dwelt within
her own skull, as though she had gone elsewhere. I
approached her very hesitantly.

"Want to come and play?"

Piquette looked at me with a sudden flash of
scorn.

"I ain't a kid," she said.

Wounded, I stamped angrily away, swearing I
would not speak to her for the rest of the summer. In
the days that followed, however, Piquette began to
interest me, and I began to want to interest her. My
reasons did not appear bizarre to me. Unlikely as it
may seem, I had only just realised that the Tonnerre
family, whom I had always heard called half-breeds,
were actually Indians, or as near as made no difference. My acquaintance with Indians was not exten-
sive. I did not remember ever having seen a real
Indian, and my new awareness that Piquette sprang
from the people of Big Bear and Poundmaker, of
Tecumseh, of the Iroquois who had eaten Father
Brebeuf's heart—all this gave her an instant attraction
in my eyes. I was a devoted reader of Pauline Johnson
at this age, and sometimes would orate aloud and in
an exalted voice, *West Wind, blow from your prairie
nest; Blow from the mountains, blow from the west*—
and so on. It seemed to me that Piquette must be in
some way a daughter of the forest, a kind of junior
prophetess of the wilds, who might impart to me, if I
took the right approach, some of the secrets which
she undoubtedly knew—where the whippoorwill made
her nest, how the coyote reared her young, or whatever it was that it said in Hiawatha.

I set about gaining Piquette's trust. She was not
allowed to go swimming, with her bad leg, but I managed to lure her down to the beach—or rather, she
came because there was nothing else to do. The water
was always icy, for the lake was fed by springs, but I
swam like a dog, thrashing my arms and legs around

at such speed and with such an output of energy that I never grew cold. Finally, when I had had enough, I came out and sat beside Piquette on the sand. When she saw me approaching, her hand squashed flat the sand castle she had been building, and she looked at me sullenly, without speaking.

"Do you like this place?" I asked, after a while, intending to lead on from there into the question of forest lore.

Piquette shrugged. "It's okay. Good as anywhere."

"I love it," I said. "We come here every summer."

"So what?" Her voice was distant, and I glanced at her uncertainly, wondering what I could have said wrong.

"Do you want to come for a walk?" I asked her. "We wouldn't need to go far. If you walk just around the point there, you come to a bay where great big reeds grow in the water, and all kinds of fish hang around there. Want to? Come on."

She shook her head.

"Your dad said I ain't supposed to do no more walking than I got to."

I tried another line.

"I bet you know a lot about the woods and all that, eh?" I began respectfully.

Piquette looked at me from her large dark unsmiling eyes.

"I don't know what in hell you're talkin' about," she replied. "You nuts or somethin'? If you mean where my old man, and me, and all them live, you better shut up, by Jesus, you hear?"

I was startled and my feelings were hurt, but I had a kind of dogged perseverance. I ignored her rebuff.

"You know something, Piquette? There's loons here, on this lake. You can see their nests just up the shore there, behind those logs. At night, you can hear them even from the cottage, but it's better to listen from the beach. My dad says we should listen and try to remember how they sound, because in a few years when more cottages are built at Diamond Lake and more people come in, the loons will go away."

Piquette was picking up stones and snail shells and then dropping them again.

"Who gives a good goddamn?" she said.

It became increasingly obvious that, as an Indian, Piquette was a dead loss. That evening I went out by myself, scrambling through the bushes that overhung the steep path, my feet slipping on the fallen spruce needles that covered the ground. When I reached the shore, I walked along the firm damp sand to the small pier that my father had built, and sat down there. I heard someone else crashing through the undergrowth and the bracken, and for a moment I thought Piquette had changed her mind, but it turned out to be my father. He sat beside me on the pier and we waited, without speaking.

At night the lake was like black glass with a streak of amber which was the path of the moon. All around, the spruce trees grew tall and close-set, branches blackly sharp against the sky, which was lightened by a cold flickering of stars. Then the loons began their calling. They rose like phantom birds from the nests on the shore, and flew out onto the dark still surface of the water.

No one can ever describe that ululating sound, the crying of the loons, and no one who has heard it can ever forget it. Plaintive, and yet with a quality of chilling mockery, those voices belonged to a world separated by aeons from our neat world of summer cottages and the lighted lamps of home.

"They must have sounded just like that," my father remarked, "before any person ever set foot here."

Then he laughed. "You could say the same, of course, about sparrows, or chipmunks, but somehow it only strikes you that way with the loons."

"I know," I said.

Neither of us suspected that this would be the last time we would ever sit here together on the shore, listening. We stayed for perhaps half an hour, and then we went back to the cottage. My mother was reading beside the fireplace. Piquette was looking at the burning birch log, and not doing anything.

"You should have come along," I said, although in fact I was glad she had not.

"Not me," Piquette said. "You wouldn' catch me walkin' way down there jus' for a bunch of squawkin' birds."

Piquette and I remained ill at ease with one another. I felt I had somehow failed my father, but I did not know what was the matter, nor why she would not or could not respond when I suggested exploring the woods or playing house. I thought it was probably her slow and difficult walking that held her back. She stayed most of the time in the cottage with my mother, helping her with the dishes or with Roddie, but hardly ever talking. Then the Duncans arrived at their cottage, and I spent my days with Mavis, who was my best friend. I could not reach Piquette at all, and I soon lost interest in trying. But all that summer she remained as both a reproach and a mystery to me.

That winter my father died of pneumonia, after less than a week's illness. For some time I saw nothing around me, being completely immersed in my own pain and my mother's. When I looked outward once more, I scarcely noticed that Piquette Tonnerre was no longer at school. I do not remember seeing her at all until four years later, one Saturday night when Mavis and I were having Cokes in the Regal Café. The jukebox was booming like tuneful thunder, and beside it, leaning lightly on its chrome and its rainbow glass, was a girl.

Piquette must have been seventeen then, although she looked about twenty. I stared at her, astounded that anyone could have changed so much. Her face, so stolid and expressionless before, was animated now with a gaiety that was almost violent. She laughed and talked very loudly with the boys around her. Her lipstick was bright carmine, and her hair was cut short and frizzily permed. She had not been pretty as a child, and she was not pretty now, for her features were still heavy and blunt. But her dark and slightly slanted eyes were beautiful, and her skin-tight skirt and orange sweater displayed to enviable advantage a soft and slender body.

She saw me, and walked over. She teetered a little, but it was not due to her once-tubercular leg, for her limp was almost gone.

"Hi, Vanessa." Her voice still had the same hoarseness. "Long time no see, eh?"

"Hi," I said. "Where've you been keeping yourself, Piquette?"

"Oh, I been around," she said. "I been away almost two years now. Been all over the place—Winnipeg, Regina, Saskatoon. Jesus, what I could tell you! I come back this summer, but I ain't stayin'. You kids goin' to the dance?"

"No," I said abruptly, for this was a sore point with me. I was fifteen, and thought I was old enough to go to the Saturday-night dances at the Flamingo. My mother, however, thought otherwise.

"Y'oughta come," Piquette said. "I never miss one. It's just about the on'y thing in this jerkwater town that's any fun. Boy, you couldn' catch me stayin' here. I don' give a shit about this place. It stinks."

She sat down beside me, and I caught the harsh over-sweetness of her perfume.

"Listen, you wanna know something, Vanessa?" she confided, her voice only slightly blurred. "Your dad was the only person in Manawaka that ever done anything good to me."

I nodded speechlessly. I was certain she was speaking the truth. I knew a little more than I had that summer at Diamond Lake, but I could not reach her now any more than I had then. I was ashamed, ashamed of my own timidity, the frightened tendency to look the other way. Yet I felt no real warmth towards her—I only felt that I ought to, because of that distant summer and because my father had hoped she would be company for me, or perhaps that I would be for her, but it had not happened that way. At this moment, meeting her again, I had to admit that she repelled and embarrassed me, and I could not help despising the self-pity in her voice. I wished she would go away. I did not want to see her. I did not know what to say to her. It seemed that we had nothing to say to one another.

"I'll tell you something else," Piquette went on. "All the old bitches an' biddies in this town will sure be surprised. I'm gettin' married this fall—my boyfriend, he's an English fella, works in the stockyards in the city there, a very tall guy, got blond wavy hair. Gee, is he ever handsome. Got this real classy name. Alvin Gerald Cummings—some handle, eh? They call him Al."

For the merest instant, then, I saw her. I really did see her, for the first and only time in all the years we had both lived in the same town. Her defiant face, momentarily, became unguarded and unmasked, and in her eyes there was a terrifying hope.

"Gee, Piquette—" I burst out awkwardly, "that's swell. That's really wonderful. Congratulations—good luck—I hope you'll be happy—"

As I mouthed the conventional phrases, I could only guess how great her need must have been, that she had been forced to seek the very things she so bitterly rejected.

When I was eighteen, I left Manawaka and went away to college. At the end of my first year, I came back home for the summer. I spent the first few days in talking non-stop with my mother, as we exchanged all the news that somehow had not found its way into letters—what had happened in my life and what had happened here in Manawaka while I was away. My mother searched her memory for events that concerned people I knew.

"Did I ever write you about Piquette Tonnerre, Vanessa?" she asked one morning.

"No, I don't think so," I replied. "Last I heard of her, she was going to marry some guy in the city. Is she still there?"

My mother looked perturbed, and it was a moment before she spoke, as though she did not know how to express what she had to tell and wished she did not need to try.

"She's dead," she said at last. Then, as I stared at her, "Oh, Vanessa, when it happened, I couldn't help thinking of her as she was that summer—so sullen and gauche and badly dressed. I couldn't help wondering if we could have done something more at that time—but what could we do? She used to be around in the cottage there with me all day, and honestly, it was all I could do to get a word out of her. She didn't even talk to your father very much, although I think she liked him in her way."

"What happened?" I asked.

"Either her husband left her, or she left him," my mother said. "I don't know which. Anyway, she came back here with two youngsters, both only babies—they must have been born very close together. She kept house, I guess, for Lazarus and her brothers, down in the valley there, in the old Tonnerre place. I used to see her on the street sometimes, but she never spoke to me. She'd put on an awful lot of weight, and she looked a mess, to tell you the truth, a real slattern, dressed any old how. She was up in court a couple of times—drunk and disorderly, of course. One Saturday night last winter, during the coldest weather, Piquette was alone in the shack with the children. The Tonnerres made home brew all the time, so I've heard, and Lazarus said later she'd been drinking most of the day when he and the boys went out that evening. They had an old woodstove there—you know the kind, with exposed pipes. The shack caught fire, Piquette didn't get out, and neither did the children."

I did not say anything. As so often with Piquette, there did not seem to be anything to say. There was a kind of silence around the image in my mind of the fire and the snow, and I wished I could put from my memory the look that I had seen once in Piquette's eyes.

I went up to Diamond Lake for a few days that summer, with Mavis and her family. The MacLeod cottage had been sold after my father's death, and I did not even go to look at it, not wanting to witness my long-ago kingdom possessed now by strangers. But one evening I went down to the shore by myself.

The small pier which my father had built was gone, and in its place there was a large and solid pier built by the government, for Galloping Mountain was now a national park, and Diamond Lake had been re-named Lake Wapakata, for it was felt that an Indian name would have a greater appeal to tourists. The one store had become several dozen, and the settlement had all the attributes of a flourishing resort—hotels, a dance-hall, cafés with neon signs, the penetrating odours of potato chips and hot dogs.

I sat on the government pier and looked out across the water. At night the lake at least was the same as it had always been, darkly shining and bearing within its black glass the streak of amber that was the path of the moon. There was no wind that evening, and everything was quiet all around me. It seemed too quiet, and then I realized that the loons were no longer here. I listened for some time, to make sure, but never once did I hear that long-drawn call, half mocking and half plaintive, spearing through the stillness across the lake.

I did not know what had happened to the birds. Perhaps they had gone away to some far place of belonging. Perhaps they had been unable to find such a place, and had simply died out, having ceased to care any longer whether they lived or not.

I remembered how Piquette had scorned to come

along, when my father and I sat there and listened to the lake birds. It seemed to me now that in some unconscious and totally unrecognised way, Piquette might have been the only one, after all, who had heard the crying of the loons.

Horses of the Night

I never knew I had distant cousins who lived up north, until Chris came down to Manawaka to go to high school. My mother said he belonged to a large family, relatives of ours, who lived at Shallow Creek, up north. I was six, and Shallow Creek seemed immeasurably far, part of a legendary winter country where no leaves grow and where the breath of seals and polar bears snuffled out steamily and turned to ice.

"Could plain people live there?" I asked my mother, meaning people who were not Eskimos. "Could there be a farm?"

"How do you mean?" she said, puzzled. "I told you. That's where they live. On the farm. Uncle Wilf—that was Chris's father, who died a few years back—he got the place as a homestead, donkey's years ago."

"But how could they grow anything? I thought you said it was up north."

"Mercy," my mother said, laughing, "it's not *that* far north, Vanessa. It's about a hundred miles beyond Galloping Mountain. You be nice to Chris, now, won't you? And don't go asking him a whole lot of questions the minute he steps inside the door."

How little my mother knew of me, I thought. Chris had been fifteen. He could be expected to feel only scorn towards me. I detested the fact that I was so young. I did not think I would be able to say anything at all to him.

"What if I don't like him?"

"What if you don't?" my mother responded sharply. "You're to watch your manners, and no acting up, understand? It's going to be quite difficult enough without that."

"Why does he have to come here, anyway?" I demanded crossly. "Why can't he go to school where he lives?"

"Because there isn't any high school up there," my mother said. "I hope he gets on well here, and isn't too homesick. Three years is a long time. It's very good of your grandfather to let him stay at the Brick House."

She said this last accusingly, as though she suspected I might be thinking differently. But I had not thought of it one way or another. We were all having dinner at the Brick House because of Chris's arrival. It was the end of August, and sweltering. My grandfather's house looked huge and cool from the outside, the high low-sweeping spruce trees shutting out the sun with their dusky out-fanned branches. But inside it wasn't cool at all. The woodstove in the kitchen was going full blast, and the whole place smelled of roasting meat.

Grandmother Connor was wearing a large mauve apron. I thought it was a nicer colour than the dark bottle-green of her dress, but she believed in wearing sombre shades lest the spirit give way to vanity, which in her case was certainly not much of a risk. The apron came up over her shapeless bosom and obscured part of her cameo brooch, the only jewellery she ever wore, with its portrait of a fiercely bearded man whom I imagined to be either Moses or God.

"Isn't it nearly time for them to be getting here, Beth?" Grandmother Connor asked.

"Train's not due until six," my mother said. "It's barely five-thirty, now. Has Father gone to the station already?"

"He went an hour ago," my grandmother said.

"He would," my mother commented.

"Now, now, Beth," my grandmother cautioned and soothed.

At last the front screen door was hurled open and

Grandfather Connor strode into the house, followed
by a tall lanky boy. Chris was wearing a white shirt, a
tie, grey trousers. I thought, unwillingly, that he looked
handsome. His face was angular, the bones showing
through the brown skin. His grey eyes were slightly
slanted, and his hair was the colour of couchgrass at
the end of summer when it has been bleached to a
light yellow by the sun. I had not planned to like him,
not even a little, but somehow I wanted to defend
him when I heard what my mother whispered to my
grandmother before they went into the front hall.

"Heavens, look at the shirt and trousers—must've
been his father's, the poor kid."

I shot out into the hall ahead of my mother, and
then stopped and stood there.

"Hi, Vanessa," Chris said.

"How come you knew who I was?" I asked.

"Well, I knew your mother and dad only had one
of a family, so I figured you must be her," he replied,
grinning.

The way he spoke did not make me feel I had
blundered. My mother greeted him warmly but shyly.
Not knowing if she were expected to kiss him or to
shake hands, she finally did neither. Grandmother
Connor, however, had no doubts. She kissed him on
both cheeks and then held him at arm's length to have
a proper look at him.

"Bless the child," she said.

Coming from anyone else, this remark would have
sounded ridiculous, especially as Chris was at least a
head taller. My grandmother was the only person I
have ever known who could say such things without
appearing false.

"I'll show you your room, Chris," my mother
offered.

Grandfather Connor, who had been standing in
the living room doorway in absolute silence, looking as
granite as a statue in the cemetery, now followed
Grandmother out to the kitchen.

"Train was forty minutes late," he said weightily.

"What a shame," my grandmother said. "But I thought it wasn't due until six, Timothy."

"Six!" my grandfather cried. "That's the mainline train. The local's due at five-twenty."

This was not correct, as both my grandmother and I knew. But neither of us contradicted him.

"What on earth are you cooking a roast for, on a night like this?" my grandfather went on. "A person could fry an egg on the sidewalk, it's that hot. Potato salad would've gone down well."

Privately I agreed with this opinion, but I could never permit myself to acknowledge agreement with him on anything. I automatically and emotionally sided with Grandmother in all issues, not because she was inevitably right but because I loved her.

"It's not a roast," my grandmother said mildly. "It's mock-duck. The stove's only been going for an hour. I thought the boy would be hungry after the trip."

My mother and Chris had come downstairs and were now in the living room. I could hear them there, talking awkwardly, with pauses.

"Potato salad," my grandfather declaimed, "would've been plenty good enough. He'd have been lucky to get it, if you ask me anything. Wilf's family hasn't got two cents to rub together. It's me that's paying for the boy's keep."

The thought of Chris in the living room, and my mother unable to explain, was too much for me. I sidled over to the kitchen door, intending to close it. But my grandmother stopped me.

"No," she said, with unexpected firmness. "Leave it open, Vanessa."

I could hardly believe it. Surely she couldn't want Chris to hear? She herself was always able to move with equanimity through a hurricane because she believed that a mighty fortress was her God. But the rest of us were not like that, and usually she did her best to protect us. At the time I felt only bewilderment. I think now that she must have realised Chris would have to learn the Brick House sooner or later, and he might as well start right away.

I had to go into the living room. I had to know how Chris would take my grandfather. Would he, as I hoped, be angry and perhaps even speak out? Or would he, meekly, only be embarrassed?

"Wilf wasn't much good, even as a young man," Grandfather Connor was trumpeting. "Nobody but a simpleton would've taken up a homestead in a place like that. Anybody could've told him that land's no use for a thing except hay."

Was he going to remind us again how well he had done in the hardware business? Nobody had ever given him a hand, he used to tell me. I am sure he believed that this was true. Perhaps it even was true.

"If the boy takes after his father, it's a poor look-out for him," my grandfather continued.

I felt the old rage of helplessness. But as for Chris—he gave no sign of feeling anything. He was sitting on the big wing-backed sofa that curled into the bay window like a black and giant seashell. He began to talk to me, quite easily, just as though he had not heard a word my grandfather was saying.

This method proved to be the one Chris always used in any dealings with my grandfather. When the bludgeoning words came, which was often, Chris never seemed, like myself, to be holding back with a terrible strained force for fear of letting go and speaking out and having the known world unimaginably fall to pieces. He would not argue or defend himself, but he did not apologise, either. He simply appeared to be absent, elsewhere. Fortunately there was very little need for response, for when Grandfather Connor pointed out your shortcomings, you were not expected to reply.

But this aspect of Chris was one which I noticed only vaguely at the time. What won me was that he would talk to me and wisecrack as though I were his same age. He was—although I didn't know the phrase then—a respecter of persons.

On the rare evenings when my parents went out, Chris would come over to mind me. These were the best times, for often when he was supposed to be doing his homework, he would make fantastic objects for my amusement, or his own—pipecleaners twisted into the shape of wildly prancing midget men, or an old set of Christmas-tree lights fixed onto a puppet theatre with a red velvet curtain that really pulled. He had skill in making miniature things of all kinds. Once for my birthday he gave me a leather saddle no bigger than a matchbox, which he had sewn himself, complete in every detail, stirrups and horn, with the criss-cross lines that were the brand name of his ranch, he said, explaining it was a reference to his own name.

"Can I go to Shallow Creek sometime?" I asked one evening.

"Sure. Some summer holidays, maybe. I've got a sister about your age. The others are all grownup."

I did not want to hear. His sisters—for Chris was the only boy—did not exist for me, not even as photographs, because I did not want them to exist. I wanted him to belong only here. Shallow Creek existed, though, no longer filled with ice mountains in my mind but as some beckoning country beyond all ordinary considerations.

"Tell me what it's like there, Chris."

"My gosh, Vanessa, I've told you before, about a thousand times."

"You never told me what your house is like."

"Didn't I? Oh well—it's made out of trees grown right there beside the lake."

"Made out of trees? Gee. Really?"

I could see it. The trees were still growing, and the leaves were firmly and greenly on them. The branches had been coaxed into formations of towers and high-up nests where you could look out and see for a hundred miles or more.

"That lake, you know," Chris said. "It's more like an inland sea. It goes on for ever and ever amen, that's how it looks. And you know what? Millions of years ago, before there were any human beings at all, that lake was full of water monsters. All different kinds of dinosaurs. Then they all died off. Nobody knows for sure why. Imagine them—all those huge creatures, with necks like snakes, and some of them had hackles on their heads, like a rooster's comb only very tough, like hard leather. Some guys from Winnipeg came up a few years back, there, and dug up dinosaur bones, and they found footprints in the rocks."

"Footprints in the *rocks?*"

"The rocks were mud, see, when the dinosaurs went trampling through, but after trillions of years the mud turned into stone and there were these mighty footprints with the claws still showing. Amazing, eh?"

I could only nod, fascinated and horrified. Imagine going swimming in those waters. What if one of the creatures had lived on?

"Tell me about the horses," I said.

"Oh, them. Well, we've got these two riding horses. Duchess and Firefly. I raised them, and you should see them. Really sleek, know what I mean? I bet I could make racers out of them."

He missed the horses, I thought with selfish satisfaction, more than he missed his family. I could visualise the pair, one sorrel and one black, swifting through all the meadows of summer.

"When can I go, Chris?"

"Well, we'll have to see. After I get through high school, I won't be at Shallow Creek much."

"Why not?"

"Because," Chris said, "what I am going to be is an engineer, civil engineer. You ever seen a really big bridge, Vanessa? Well, I haven't either, but I've seen pictures. You take the Golden Gate Bridge in San Francisco, now. Terrifically high—all those thin ribs of steel, joined together to go across this very wide stretch of water. It doesn't seem possible, but it's there. That's what engineers do. Imagine doing something like that, eh?"

I could not imagine it. It was beyond me.

"Where will you go?" I asked. I did not want to think of his going anywhere.

"Winnipeg, to college," he said with assurance.

The Depression did not get better, as everyone had been saying it would. It got worse, and so did the drought. That part of the prairies where we lived was never dustbowl country. The farms around Manawaka never had a total crop failure, and afterwards, when the drought was over, people used to remark on this fact proudly, as though it had been due to some virtue or special status, like the Children of Israel being afflicted by Jehovah but never in real danger of annihilation. But although Manawaka never knew the worst, what it knew was bad enough. Or so I learned later. At the time I saw none of it. For me, the Depression and drought were external and abstract, malevolent gods whose names I secretly learned although they were concealed from me, and whose evil I sensed only superstitiously, knowing they threatened us but not how or why. What I really saw was only what went on in our family.

"He's done quite well all through, despite everything," my mother said. She sighed, and I knew she was talking about Chris.

"I know," my father said. "We've been over all this before, Beth. But quite good just isn't good enough. Even supposing he managed to get a scholarship, which isn't likely, it's only tuition and books. What about room and board? Who's going to pay for that? Your father?"

"I see I shouldn't have brought up the subject at all," my mother said in an aloof voice.

"I'm sorry," my father said impatiently. "But you know, yourself, he's the only one who might possibly—"

"I can't bring myself to ask Father about it, Ewen. I simply cannot do it."

"There wouldn't be much point in asking," my father said, "when the answer is a foregone conclusion. He feels he's done his share, and actually, you know, Beth, he has, too. Three years, after all. He may not have done it gracefully, but he's done it."

We were sitting in the living room, and it was evening. My father was slouched in the grey armchair that was always his. My mother was slenderly straight-backed in the blue chair in which nobody else ever sat. I was sitting on the footstool, beige needlepoint with mathematical roses, to which I had staked my own claim. This seating arrangement was obscurely satis-factory to me, perhaps because predictable, like the three bears. I was pretending to be colouring into a scribbler on my knee, and from time to time my lethargic purple crayon added a feather to an out-landish swan. To speak would be to invite dismissal. But their words forced questions in my head.

"Chris isn't going away, is he?"

My mother swooped, shocked at her own neglect.

"My heavens—are you still up, Vanessa? What am I thinking of?"

"Where is Chris going?"

"We're not sure yet," my mother evaded, chivvy-ing me up the stairs. "We'll see."

He would not go, I thought. Something would happen, miraculously, to prevent him. He would re-main, with his long loping walk and his half-slanted grey eyes and his talk that never excluded me. He would stay right here. And soon, because I desperately wanted to, and because every day mercifully made me older, quite soon I would be able to reply with such a lightning burst of knowingness that it would astound him, when he spoke of the space or was it some black sky that never ended anywhere beyond this earth. Then I would not be innerly belittled for being unable to figure out what he would best like to hear. At that good and imagined time, I would not any longer be limited. I would not any longer be young.

I was nine when Chris left Manawaka. The day before he was due to go, I knocked on the door of his room in the Brick House.

"Come in," Chris said. "I'm packing. Do you know how to fold socks, Vanessa?"

"Sure. Of course."

"Well, get folding on that bunch there, then."

I had come to say goodbye, but I did not want to say it yet. I got to work on the socks. I did not intend to speak about the matter of college, but the knowledge that I must not speak about it made me uneasy. I was afraid I would blurt out a reference to it in my anxiety not to. My mother had said, "He's taken it amazingly well—he doesn't even mention it, so we mustn't either."

"Tomorrow night you'll be in Shallow Creek," I ventured.

"Yeh." He did not look up. He went on stuffing clothes and books into his suitcase.

"I bet you'll be glad to see the horses, eh?" I wanted him to say he didn't care about the horses any more and that he would rather stay here.

"It'll be good to see them again," Chris said. "Mind handing over those socks now, Vanessa? I think I can just squash them in at the side here. Thanks. Hey, look at that, will you? Everything's in. Am I an expert packer or am I an expert packer?"

I sat on his suitcase for him so it would close, and then he tied a piece of rope around it because the lock wouldn't lock.

"Ever thought what it would be like to be a traveller, Vanessa?" he asked.

I thought of Richard Halliburton, taking an elephant over the Alps and swimming illicitly in the Taj Mahal lily pool by moonlight.

"It would be keen," I said, because this was the word Chris used to describe the best possible. "That's what I'm going to do someday."

He did not say, as for a moment I feared he might, that girls could not be travellers.

"Why not?" he said. "Sure you will, if you really want to. I got this theory, see, that anybody can do anything at all, anything, if they really set their minds to it. But you have to have this total concentration. You have to focus on it with your whole mental powers, and not let it slip away by forgetting to hold it in your mind. If you hold it in your mind, like, then it's real, see? You take most people, now. They can't concentrate worth a darn."

"Do you think I can?" I enquired eagerly, believing that this was what he was talking about.

"What?" he said. "Oh—sure. Sure I think you can. Naturally."

Chris did not write after he left Manawaka. About a month later we had a letter from his mother. He was not at Shallow Creek. He had not gone back. He had got off the northbound train at the first stop after Manawaka, cashed in his ticket, and thumbed a lift with a truck to Winnipeg. He had written to his mother from there, but had given no address. She had not heard from him since. My mother read Aunt Tess's letter aloud to my father. She was too upset to care whether I was listening or not.

"I can't think what possessed him, Ewen. He never seemed irresponsible. What if something should happen to him? What if he's broke? What do you think we should do?"

"What can we do? He's nearly eighteen. What he does is his business. Simmer down, Beth, and let's decide what we're going to tell your father."

"Oh Lord," my mother said. "There's that to consider, of course."

I went out without either of them noticing. I walked to the hill at the edge of the town, and down into the valley where the scrub oak and poplar grew almost to the banks of the Wachakwa River. I found the oak where we had gone last autumn, in a gang, to smoke cigarettes made of dried leaves and pieces of newspaper. I climbed to the lowest branch and stayed there for a while.

I was not consciously thinking about Chris. I was not thinking of anything. But when at last I cried, I felt relieved afterwards and could go home again.

Chris departed from my mind, after that, with a quickness that was due to the other things that happened. My Aunt Edna, who was a secretary in Winnipeg, returned to Manawaka to live because the insurance company cut down on staff and she could not find another job. I was intensely excited and jubilant about her return, and could not see why my mother seemed the opposite, even though she was as fond of Aunt Edna as I was. Then my brother Roderick was born, and that same year Grandmother Connor died. The strangeness, the unbelievability, of both these events took up all of me.

When I was eleven, almost two years after Chris had left, he came back without warning. I came home from school and found him sitting in our living room. I could not accept that I had nearly forgotten him until this instant. Now that he was present, and real again, I felt I had betrayed him by not thinking of him more.

He was wearing a navy-blue serge suit. I was old enough now to notice that it was a cheap one and had been worn a considerable time. Otherwise, he looked the same, the same smile, the same knife-boned face with no flesh to speak of, the same unresting eyes.

"How come you're here?" I cried. "Where have you been, Chris?"

"I'm a traveller," he said. "Remember?"

He was a traveller all right. One meaning of the word *traveller* in our part of the world, was a travelling salesman. Chris was selling vacuum cleaners. That evening he brought out his line and showed us.

He went through his spiel for our benefit, so we could hear how it sounded.

"Now, look, Beth," he said, turning the appliance on and speaking loudly above its moaning roar, "see how it brightens up this old rug of yours? Keen, eh?"

"Wonderful," my mother laughed. "Only we can't afford one."

"Oh well—" Chris said quickly. "I'm not trying to sell one to you. I'm only showing you. Listen, I've only been in this job a month, but I figure this is really a going thing. I mean, it's obvious, isn't it? You take all those old wire carpet-beaters of yours, Beth. You could kill yourself over them and your carpet isn't going to look one-tenth as good as it does with this."

"Look, I don't want to seem—" my father put in, "but, hell, they're not exactly a new invention, and we're not the only ones who can't afford—"

"This is a pretty big outfit, you know?" Chris insisted. "Listen, I don't plan to stay, Ewen. But a guy could work at it for a year or so, and save—right? Lots of guys work their way through university like that."

I needed to say something really penetrating, something that would show him I knew the passionate truth of his conviction.

"I bet—" I said, "I bet you'll sell a thousand, Chris."

Two years ago, this statement would have seemed self-evident, unquestionable. Yet now, when I had spoken, I knew that I did not believe it.

The next time Chris visited Manawaka, he was selling magazines. He had the statistics worked out. If every sixth person in town would get a subscription to *Country Guide*, he could make a hundred dollars in a month. We didn't learn how he got on. He didn't stay in Manawaka a full month. When he turned up again, it was winter. Aunt Edna phoned.

"Nessa? Listen, kiddo, tell your mother she's to come down if it's humanly possible. Chris is here, and Father's having fits."

So in five minutes we were scurrying through the

snow, my mother and I, with our overshoes not even properly done up and our feet getting wet. We need not have worried. By the time we reached the Brick House, Grandfather Connor had retired to the basement, where he sat in the rocking chair beside the furnace, making occasional black pronouncements like a subterranean oracle. These loud utterances made my mother and aunt wince, but Chris didn't seem to notice any more than he ever had. He was engrossed in telling us about the mechanism he was holding. It had a cranker handle like an old-fashioned sewing machine.

"You attach the ball of wool here, see? Then you set this little switch here, and adjust this lever, and you're away to the races. Neat, eh?"

It was a knitting machine. Chris showed us the finished products. The men's socks he had made were coarse wool, one pair in grey heather and another in maroon. I was impressed.

"Gee—can I do it, Chris?"

"Sure. Look, you just grab hold of the handle right here."

"Where did you get it?" my mother asked.

"I've rented it. The way I figure it, Beth, I can sell these things at about half the price you'd pay in a store, and they're better quality."

"Who are you going to sell them to?" Aunt Edna enquired.

"You take all these guys who do outside work—they need heavy socks all year round, not just in winter. I think this thing could be quite a gold mine."

"Before I forget," my mother said, "how's your mother and the family keeping?"

"They're okay," Chris said in a restrained voice. "They're not short of hands, if that's what you mean, Beth. My sisters have their husbands there."

Then he grinned, casting away the previous moment, and dug into his suitcase.

"Hey, I haven't shown you—these are for you, Vanessa, and this pair is for Roddie."

My socks were cherry-coloured. The very small ones for my brother were turquoise.

Chris only stayed until after dinner, and then he went away again.

After my father died, the whole order of life was torn. Nothing was known or predictable any longer. For months I lived almost entirely within myself, so when my mother told me one day that Chris couldn't find any work at all because there were no jobs and so he had gone back to Shallow Creek to stay, it made scarcely any impression on me. But that summer, my mother decided I ought to go away for a holiday. She hoped it might take my mind off my father's death. What, if anything, was going to take her mind off his death, she did not say.

"Would you like to go to Shallow Creek for a week or so?" she asked me. "I could write to Chris's mother."

Then I remembered, all in a torrent, the way I had imagined it once, when he used to tell me about it—the house fashioned of living trees, the lake like a sea where monsters had dwelt, the grass that shone like green wavering light while the horses flew in the splendour of their pride.

"Yes," I said. "Write to her."

The railway did not go through Shallow Creek, but Chris met me at Challoner's Crossing. He looked different, not only thinner, but—what was it? Then I saw that it was the fact that his face and neck were tanned red-brown, and he was wearing denims, farm pants, and a blue plaid shirt open at the neck. I liked him like this. Perhaps the change was not so much in him as in myself, now that I was thirteen. He looked masculine in a way I had not been aware of, before.

"C'mon, kid," he said. "The limousine's over here."

It was a wagon and two horses, which was what I had expected, but the nature of each was not what I had expected. The wagon was a long and clumsy one, made of heavy planking, and the horses were both plough horses, thick in the legs, and badly matched as a team. The mare was short and stout, matronly. The gelding was very tall and gaunt, and he limped.

"Allow me to introduce you," Chris said. "Floss—Trooper—this is Vanessa."

He did not mention the other horses, Duchess and Firefly, and neither did I, not all the fortnight I was there. I guess I had known for some years now, without realising it, that the pair had only ever existed in some other dimension.

Shallow Creek wasn't a town. It was merely a name on a map. There was a grade school a few miles away, but that was all. They had to go to Challoner's Crossing for their groceries. We reached the farm, and Chris steered me through the crowd of aimless cows and wolfish dogs in the yard, while I flinched with panic.

It was perfectly true that the house was made out of trees. It was a fair-sized but elderly shack, made out of poplar poles and chinked with mud. There was an upstairs, which was not so usual around here, with three bedrooms, one of which I was to share with Chris's sister, Jeannie, who was slightly younger than I, a pallid-eyed girl who was either too shy to talk or who had nothing to say. I never discovered which, because I was so reticent with her myself, wanting to push her away, not to recognise her, and at the same time experiencing a shocked remorse at my own unacceptable feelings.

Aunt Tess, Chris's mother, was severe in manner and yet wanting to be kind, worrying over it, making tentative overtures which were either ignored or repelled by her older daughters and their monosyllabic husbands. Youngsters swam in and out of the house like shoals of nameless fishes. I could not see how so many people could live here, under the one roof, but then I learned they didn't. The married daughters had their own dwelling places, nearby, but some kind of communal life was maintained. They wrangled end-lessly but they never left one another alone, not even for a day.

Chris took no part at all, none. When he spoke, it was usually to the children, and they would often fol-low him around the yard or to the barn, not pestering but just trailing along in clusters of three or four. He never told them to go away. I liked him for this, but it bothered me, too. I wished he would return his sis-ters' bickering for once, or tell them to clear out, or even yell at one of the kids. But he never did. He closed himself off from squabbling voices just as he used to do with Grandfather Connor's spearing words.

The house had no screens on the doors or win-dows, and at meal times the flies were so numerous you could hardly see the food for the iridescent-winged blue-black bodies squirming all over it. No-body noticed my squeamishness except Chris, and he was the only one from whom I really wanted to con-ceal it.

"Fan with your hand," he murmured.

"It's okay," I said quickly.

For the first time in all the years we had known each other, we could not look the other in the eye. Around the table, the children stabbed and snivelled, until Chris's oldest sister, driven frantic, shrieked, *Shut up shut up shut up.* Chris began asking me about Manawaka then, as though nothing were going on around him.

They were due to begin haying, and Chris an-nounced that he was going to camp out in the bluff near the hayfields. To save himself the long drive in the wagon each morning, he explained, but I felt this wasn't the real reason.

"Can I go, too?" I begged. I could not bear the thought of living in the house with all the others who were not known to me, and Chris not here.

"Well, I don't know—"

"Please. Please, Chris. I won't be any trouble. I promise."

Finally he agreed. We drove out in the big hayrack, its slatted sides rattling, its old wheels jolting metallically. The road was narrow and dirt, and around it the low bushes grew, wild rose and blueberry and wolf willow with silver leaves. Sometimes we would come to a bluff of pale-leaved poplar trees and once a red-winged blackbird flew up out of the branches and into the hot dusty blue of the sky.

Then we were there. The hayfields lay beside the lake. It was my first view of the water which had spawned saurian giants so long ago. Chris drove the hayrack through the fields of high coarse grass and on down almost to the lake's edge, where there was no shore but only the green rushes like floating meadows in which the water birds nested. Beyond the undulating reeds the open lake stretched, deep, green-grey, out and out, beyond sight.

No human word could be applied. The lake was not lonely or untamed. These words relate to people, and there was nothing of people here. There was no feeling about the place. It existed in some world in which man was not yet born. I looked at the grey reaches of it and felt threatened. It was like the view of God which I had held since my father's death. Distant, indestructible, totally indifferent.

Chris had jumped down off the hayrack.

"We're not going to camp *here,* are we?" I asked and pleaded.

"No. I just want to let the horses drink. We'll camp up there in the bluff."

I looked. "It's still pretty close to the lake, isn't it?"

"Don't worry," Chris said, laughing. "You won't get your feet wet."

"I didn't mean that."

Chris looked at me.

"I know you didn't," he said. "But let's learn to be a little tougher, and not let on, eh? It's necessary."

Chris worked through the hours of sun, while I lay on the half-formed stack of hay and looked up at the sky. The blue air trembled and spun with the heat haze, and the hay on which I was lying held the scents of grass and dust and wild mint.

In the evening, Chris took the horses to the lake again, and then he drove the hayrack to the edge of the bluff and we spread out our blankets underneath it. He made a fire and we had coffee and a tin of stew, and then we went to bed. We did not wash, and we slept in our clothes. It was only when I was curled up uncomfortably with the itching blanket around me that I felt a sense of unfamiliarity at being here, with Chris only three feet away, a self-consciousness I would not have felt even the year before. I do not think he felt this sexual strangeness. If he wanted me not to be a child—and he did—it was not with the wish that I would be a woman. It was something else.

"Are you asleep, Vanessa?" he asked.

"No. I think I'm lying on a tree root."

"Well, shift yourself, then," he said. "Listen, kid, I never said anything before, because I didn't really know what to say, but—you know how I felt about your dad dying, and that, don't you?"

"Yes," I said chokingly. "It's okay. I know."

"I used to talk with Ewen sometimes. He didn't see what I was driving at, mostly, but he'd always listen, you know? You don't find many guys like that."

We were both silent for a while.

"Look," Chris said finally. "Ever noticed how much brighter the stars are when you're completely away from any houses? Even the lamps up at the farm, there make enough of a glow to keep you from seeing properly like you can out here. What do they make you think about, Vanessa?"

"Well—"

"I guess most people don't give them much thought at all, except maybe to say—*very pretty*—or like that. But the point is, they aren't like that. The stars and planets, in themselves, are just not like that, not *pretty*, for heaven's sake. They're gigantic—some of them burning—imagine those worlds tearing through space and made of pure fire. Or the ones that are absolutely dead—just rock or ice and no warmth in them. There must be some, though, that have living creatures. You wonder what *they* could look like, and what they feel. We won't ever get to know. But somebody will know, someday. I really believe that. Do you ever think about this kind of thing at all?"

He was twenty-one. The distance between us was still too great. For years I had wanted to be older so I might talk with him, but now I felt unready.

"Sometimes," I said, hesitantly, making it sound like *Never*.

"People usually say there must be a God," Chris went on, "because otherwise how did the universe get here? But that's ridiculous. If the stars and planets go on to infinity, they could have existed forever, for no reason at all. Maybe they weren't ever created. Look—what's the alternative? To believe in a God who is brutal. What else could He be? You've only got to look anywhere around you. It would be an insult to Him to believe in a God like that. Most people don't like talking about this kind of thing—it embarrasses them, you know? Or else they're not interested. I don't mind. I can always think about things myself. You don't actually need anyone to talk to. But about God, though—if there's a war, like it looks there will be, would people claim that was planned? What kind of a God would pull a trick like that? And yet, you know, plenty of guys would think it was a godsend, and who's to say they're wrong? It would be a job, and you'd get around and see places."

He paused, as though waiting for me to say something. When I did not, he resumed.

"Ewen told me about the last war, once. He hardly ever talked about it, but this once he told me about seeing the horses in the mud, actually going under, you know? And the way their eyes looked when they realised they weren't going to get out. Ever seen horses' eyes when they're afraid, I mean really berserk with fear, like in a bush-fire? Ewen said a guy tended to concentrate on the horses because he didn't dare think what was happening to the men. Including himself. Do you ever listen to the news at all, Vanessa?"

"I—"

I could only feel how foolish I must sound, still unable to reply as I would have wanted, comprehendingly. I felt I had failed myself utterly. I could not speak even the things I knew. As for the other things, the things I did not know, I resented Chris's facing me with them. I took refuge in pretending to be asleep, and after a while Chris stopped talking.

Chris left Shallow Creek some months after the war began, and joined the Army. After his basic training he was sent to England. We did not hear from him until about a year later, when a letter arrived for me.

"Vanessa—what's wrong?" my mother asked.

"Nothing."

"Don't fib," she said firmly. "What did Chris say in his letter, honey?"

"Oh—not much."

She gave me a curious look and then she went away. She would never have demanded to see the letter. I did not show it to her and she did not ask about it again.

Six months later my mother heard from Aunt Tess. Chris had been sent home from England and discharged from the Army because of a mental breakdown. He was now in the provincial mental hospital and they did not know how long he would have to remain there. He had been violent, before, but now he was not violent. He was, the doctors had told his mother, passive.

Violent. I could not associate the word with Chris, who had been so much the reverse. I could not bear to consider what anguish must have catapulted him into that even greater anguish. But the way he was now seemed almost worse. How might he be? Sitting quite still, wearing the hospital's grey dressing-gown, the animation gone from his face?

My mother cared about him a great deal, but her immediate thought was not for him.

"When I think of you, going up to Shallow Creek that time," she said, "and going out camping with him, and what might have happened—"

I, also, was thinking of what might have happened. But we were not thinking of the same thing. For the first time I recognised, at least a little, the dimensions of his need to talk that night. He must have understood perfectly well how impossible it would be, with a thirteen-year-old. But there was no one else. All his life's choices had grown narrower and narrower. He had been forced to return to the alien lake of home, and when finally he saw a means of getting away, it could only be into a turmoil which appalled him and which he dreaded even more than he knew. I had listened to his words, but I had not really heard them, not until now. It would not have made much difference to what happened, but I wished it were not too late to let him know.

Once when I was on holiday from college, my mother got me to help her clean out the attic. We sifted through boxes full of junk, old clothes, school-books, bric-a-brac that once had been treasures. In one of the boxes I found the miniature saddle that Chris had made for me a long time ago.

"Have you heard anything recently?" I asked, ashamed that I had not asked sooner.

She glanced up at me. "Just the same. It's always the same. They don't think there will be much improvement."

Then she turned away.

"He always used to seem so—hopeful. Even when there was really nothing to be hopeful about. That's what I find so strange. He *seemed* hopeful, didn't you think?"

"Maybe it wasn't hope," I said.

"How do you mean?"

I wasn't certain myself. I was thinking of all the schemes he'd had, the ones that couldn't possibly have worked, the unreal solutions to which he'd clung because there were no others, the brave and useless strokes of fantasy against a depression that was both the world's and his own.

"I don't know," I said. "I just think things were always more difficult for him than he let on, that's all. Remember that letter?"

"Yes."

"Well—what it said was that they could force his body to march and even to kill, but what they didn't know was that he'd fooled them. He didn't live inside it any more."

"Oh, Vanessa—" my mother said. "You must have suspected right then."

"Yes, but—"

I could not go on, could not say that the letter seemed only the final heartbreaking extension of that way he'd always had of distancing himself from the absolute unbearability of battle.

I picked up the tiny saddle and turned it over in my hand.

"Look. His brand, the name of his ranch. The Criss-Cross."

"What ranch?" my mother said, bewildered.

"The one where he kept his racing horses. Duchess and Firefly."

Some words came into my head, a single line from a poem I had once heard. I knew it referred to a lover who did not want the morning to come, but to me it had another meaning, a different relevance.

Slowly, slowly, horses of the night—

The night must move like this for him, slowly, all through the days and nights. I could not know whether the land he journeyed through was inhabited by terrors, the old monster-kings of the lake, or whether

he had discovered at last a way for himself to make
the necessary dream perpetual.

I put the saddle away once more, gently and
ruthlessly, back into the cardboard box.

The Half-Husky

When Peter Chorniuk's wagon clanked slowly into our back yard that September, it never occurred to me that this visit would be different from any other. Peter Chorniuk lived at Galloping Mountain, a hundred miles north of Manawaka, and he was one of the few men from whom it was still possible to buy birch, for the trees were getting scarce. Every autumn he came down to Manawaka and brought a load of birch for our furnace. Birch held the fire better than poplar, but it was expensive and we could afford only the one load, so my grandfather burned a mixture. I watched the man whoa the team and then climb onto the back of the wagon and begin throwing down the cordwood sticks. The powdery white bark was still on and in places had been torn, exposing the pale rust colour of the inner bark. The logs thudded dryly as he flung them down. Later my grandfather and I would have to carry them inside. The plebeian poplar was kept outside, but the birch was stacked in the basement.

I was lying on the roof of the tool-shed, reading. An enormous spruce tree grew beside the shed, and the branches feathered out across the roof, concealing anyone who was perched there. I was fifteen, and getting too old to be climbing on roofs, my mother said.

"Hi, Mr. Chorniuk," I called.

He looked up, and I emerged from the spruce boughs and waved at him. He grinned.

"Hi, Vanessa. Listen, you want a dog, eh?"

"What?" I said. "Has Natasha had pups again?"

"Yeh, that's right," Mr. Chorniuk said. "There's no stopping Natasha. This is her fifth litter. This time she got herself mixed up with a Husky."

"Gee." I was impressed. "The pups are half-Husky? What're they like?"

"Come and see," he beckoned. "I brought one for you."

I slid quickly down from the tool-shed roof onto the fence and then to the ground. The pup was in a cardboard box in the front of the wagon. It was very young and plump, and its fur was short and soft, almost like the down on a chick. It was black, like Natasha, but it had a ruff of white at its throat, and white markings on its head. I picked it up, and it struggled in annoyance, trying to escape, then settled down and sniffed my hands to see if I was friendly.

"Can I really have it?" I asked.

"Sure," Mr. Chorniuk said. "You'll be doing me a favor. What am I going to do with six of them? Everybody up at the mountain's got all the dogs they got any use for. I can't drown them. My wife says I'm crazy. But I'd as soon drown a kid, to tell you the truth. Will your mom let you keep it?"

"Oh sure, *she* will. But—"

"Think *he* won't?" Mr. Chorniuk said, meaning Grandfather Connor. My mother and brother and I had lived in the Brick House with my grandfather ever since the death of my father.

"Well, we'll soon know," I said. "Here he comes now."

Grandfather Connor came striding out of the house. He was in his late eighties, but he walked straight, carrying his bulky body with an energy that was partly physical and partly sheer determination. His splendid condition, for a man of his age, he attributed to unceasing toil and good habits. He touched neither tobacco nor snuff, he spurned playing cards, and he based his drinking of only tea on the Almighty's contention that wine was a mocker and strong drink was raging. It was a warm day, the leaves turning a clear lemon yellow on the Manitoba maples and the late afternoon sun lighting up the windows of the Brick House like silver foil, but my grandfather was wearing his grey-heather sweater buttoned up to the neck. His face was set in its accustomed expression of displeasure, but it was still a handsome face—strong heavy features, a beaked nose, eyes a chilled blue like snow-shadows.

"Well, Peter, you've brought the wood." It was his habit to begin conversations with a statement of the obvious, so that nothing except agreement was possible.

"Yep. Here it is."

"How much will it be this time?" Grandfather Connor asked.

Mr. Chorniuk told him the price and my grandfather looked stricken. He had never accepted the fact that he could not buy anything for what he paid forty years ago, so he had the permanent conviction that he was being cheated. He began to argue, and Mr. Chorniuk's face assumed a look of purposeful blankness. Just then my grandfather noticed the dog.

"What's that you've got there, Vanessa?"

"Mr. Chorniuk says I can have it, Grandfather. Can I? I promise I'll look after it myself. It wouldn't be any trouble."

"We don't want no dogs around the place," my grandfather said. "They're messy and they're destructive. You'd only be making work for your mother. You might consider her for a change."

"If she says I can, though?" I persisted.

"There's no *if* about it," he decreed flatly.

"Part Husky, that one," Mr. Chorniuk put in, trying to be helpful. "He'd make a good watch dog. Nor worry about pups. It's a him."

"Husky!" Grandfather Connor exclaimed. "I wouldn't trust one of them things as far as I could see it. Tear Roddie to bits, more than likely."

My brother Roderick was five and a half and exceptionally fond of animals. I was pointing this out, arguing hotly and passionately and with no more tact than my grandfather himself, when Roddie and my mother came out into the yard. My brother, sizing up the situation rapidly, added his pleas to mine.

"Aw, come on, Grandfather. Please."

"Can I, Mother?" I begged. "I'll look after him. You won't have to do a thing. Cross my heart."

My mother was always torn between her children and a desire not to provoke my grandfather.

"Well, it's all right as far as I'm concerned," she said uncertainly, "but—"

What made my grandfather finally and untypically change his mind was the delay involved.

"Take the blamed thing away, then, Vanessa, for mercy's sake, or this wood won't get unloaded before tomorrow morning. But he's only to go in the basement, mind. If I catch him in the rest of the house, you'll have to get rid of him, understand?"

"Yes, yes!" I fled with the pup. My brother followed.

The pup explored the basement, snuffling around the crate of apples on the floor, burrowing behind the sacks of potatoes and turnips, falling over his own infant-clumsy feet in his attempt to scurry in every direction at once. Roddie and I laughed at him, and then I picked him up to try him in his new bed and he nervously wet all over the blanket.

"What're we going to call him, Vanessa?"

I pondered. Then the name came to me.

"Nanuk."

"*Na-nook?* That's not a name."

"It's an Eskimo name, dopey," I said abruptly.

"Is it really?"

"Sure it is." I had no idea whether it was or not. "Anybody knows that."

"You think you're so smart," my brother said, offended.

"What would you suggest, then?" I asked sarcastically.

"Well, I was thinking of Laddie."

"Laddie! What! A corny old name like that?"

Then I became aware that my own voice carried some disturbing echo of my grandfather's.

"Listen, Laddie's okay for a collie or like that," I amended, "but this one's got to have an Eskimo name, on account of his father being a Husky, see?"

"Yeh, maybe so," my brother said. "Here, Nanuk!"

The pup did not even look up. He seemed too young to own any kind of a name.

Harvey Shinwell delivered our papers. He was a heavily built boy of about sixteen, with colourless eyebrows and a pallid mottled face. After school he would go and pick up the papers from the station and deliver them on his old bicycle. He was somebody who had always been around and whom I had never actually seen. Until that winter.

Nanuk had the run of the yard, but the gates were kept closed. The picket fence was high, and the wooden pieces were driven deep into the earth, so Nanuk could neither get over nor tunnel under. I took him out on walks with me but apart from that he stayed in the yard. This did not mean he was too much confined, however, for our yard was nearly an acre. One day I got home from school just as Harvey Shinwell had come to the gate and thrown the Winnipeg *Free Press* onto our front porch. He didn't get back on his bike immediately. He was standing at the gate, and when I approached along the sidewalk I could see what he was doing.

In his hand he held a short pointed stick. He was poking it through the bars of the gate. On the other side was Nanuk, only four months old, but snarling in a way I had never heard before. He was trying to catch the stick with his teeth, but Harvey withdrew it too quickly. Then Harvey jabbed it in again, and this time it caught Nanuk in the face. He yelped with the pain of it, but he was not driven away. He came back again, trying to get hold of the stick, and once more Harvey with a calm deliberation drove the wooden javelin at the dog.

"What do you think you're doing?" I yelled. "You leave my dog alone, you hear?"

Harvey looked up with a lethargic grin and mounted his bike.

"He tried to bite me," he said. "He's dangerous."

"He is not!" I cried, infuriated. "I saw!"

"Why don't you run and tell your mother, then?" Harvey said, in phony falsetto.

I went inside the yard and knelt in the snow beside Nanuk. He was getting too big for me to lift him. He seemed to have forgotten about the stick. He welcomed me in his usual way, jumping up, taking my wrist gently between his jaws and pretending to bite but holding it so carefully that he never left even the faint marks of his teeth.

I forgot about the stick then, also. Nanuk was enough of a problem because of my grandfather. Their paths hardly ever crossed, but this was only due to the organisational abilities of my mother, who was constantly removing the dog to some place where my grandfather wasn't. Sometimes she would complain irritably about this extra responsibility—"If I'd ever realised, Vanessa, how much work this creature would mean, I'd never have agreed—" and so on. Then I would feel wounded and resentful, and could scarcely bear the fact that the trouble the dog caused her was my fault.

"Okay, give him away," I would storm. "See if I care. Have him chloroformed."

"Maybe I will, then, one of these days," my mother would reply stonily, "and it would serve you right for talking like a lunatic and saying things you don't mean."

Having scared each other more than either of us intended, we would both give in.

"He's really very good," my mother would admit. "And he's company during the day for Roddie."

"Are you sure?" No amount of assurance was ever enough for me. "Are you quite sure you wouldn't rather—"

"Oh yes, of course. It'll be all right, Vanessa. We mustn't worry."

"Yes. Okay," I would say. "We won't, then."

And we would both go our perpetually worrying ways.

Some months later I happened once more to come home just at the moment when Harvey was delivering the paper. This time I saw him from half a block away, and walked along the sidewalk quietly, sticking close to the caragana hedges for concealment. He had half a doughnut in one hand, and in the other a white envelope. He held the doughnut through the iron grille, and when Nanuk came up to the gate, he opened the envelope.

Nanuk screamed. The sound was so sudden and acute that my breath was forced back in upon my lungs. I wondered how many times some kind of tormenting had taken place. I felt the burden of my own neglect. I should have taken it seriously before. I should have watched out for it.

Harvey rode off. When I went to Nanuk and finally calmed him enough to touch him, I found traces of the pepper around his still-closed eyes.

Whenever I tried to work out a plan of counter-attack, my rage would spin me into fantasy—Harvey, fallen into the deepest part of the Wachakwa River, unable to swim, and Nanuk, capable of rescue but waiting for a signal from me. Would I speak or not? Sometimes I let Harvey drown. Sometimes at the last minute I spared him—this was more satisfactory than his death, as it enabled me to feel great-hearted while at the same time enjoying a continuing revenge in the form of Harvey's gibbering remorse. But none of this was much use except momentarily, and when the flamboyant theatre of my mind grew empty again, I still did not know what to do in reality.

I did not tell my mother. I could not face her look of distracted exhaustion at being presented with something else that she was expected to solve and did not know how any more than I. Also, I could not forget

what Harvey had said—"Why don't you run and tell
your mother?" I began hurrying home from school, so
I would get there first. I thought he would not do anything if I were there.

Harvey flipped the newspaper neatly onto the
front porch. It landed just at my elbow. I was sitting
on the top step. Nanuk was at the gate. I called to
him, but he did not seem to hear.

Nanuk was eight months old now, and fully
grown. He had changed utterly. His black fur had
grown and coarsened, losing the downy quality it
used to have, but gaining a marvellous sheen. It rip-
pled silkily across the powerful shoulders that showed
the Husky strain in him. The white ruff on his throat
and chest was like a lion's plumage. He had a Husky's
up-pointed ears and slanted eyes, and his jaws were
wolfish.

He was growling now, a deep low sound. Not
merely a warning—an open declaration of enmity. He
did not try to get over the gate. He remained at a
slight distance, his lips drawn back in the devil's grin
which I had only seen in pictures of other dogs of
his blood, never on Nanuk. Harvey glanced at me,
and his face puckered into a smile. He knew he was
safe on the other side of the fence. Then, with a speed
which caught me off guard, he pulled out a slingshot.
The stone was fired before I could get down the steps
and as far as the gate. It hit Nanuk on the throat,
where his fur was thick. It did not damage him much,
but it drove him wild. He flung himself against the
bars of the gate. Harvey was already on his bicycle
and pedalling away.

I grabbed the gate handle. Beside me, Nanuk
was in a frenzy to get out. He could probably have
caught up with the bicycle.

I looked at Nanuk's unrecognisable face, at the
fur rising in hackles along the top of his back, at the
demented eyes. My hand clenched the gate shut once
more. I walked back into the house without looking
again at the dog. I went to my room and locked the

door. I did not want to see anyone, or talk. I had realised something for the first time. Nanuk had all the muscular force and all the equipment he needed to kill a man. In that second, I had not been sure that he would not do it.

Now I had to tell my mother. She did try, after that, to keep Nanuk inside the house at the time when Harvey delivered the papers. But something was always going wrong. Grandfather Connor let the dog out, claiming that Nanuk was giving the house a foul smell. Or else my mother forgot, and would be apologetic, and this would make me feel worse than if she had said nothing at all.

I tried to get home from school early, but I often forgot and went with my friends to the Regal Café to play the jukebox and drink coffee. On the days when I remembered and put Nanuk safely in the basement, I would watch from the bay window of the living room and see Harvey deposit the paper on the porch. He looked in through the gate, and sometimes he even parked his bike for a moment and waited, to make sure the dog was not there. Then, with an exaggerated shrug, as though he knew he were being observed, he would ride off, his face expressionless.

When I was late, sometimes my brother would report to me.

"Nanuk was out today, Vanessa," he told me one afternoon. "Mum wasn't home. And he wouldn't come when I called him."

"What happened?"

"Harvey—well, he lit a whole bunch of matches all together," my brother said, "and dropped them. I got some water, after, and put it on Nanuk's head. He wasn't burned much, Vanessa, honestly."

I no longer wove intricate dreams in which I either condemned Harvey or magnanimously spared him. What I felt now was not complicated at all. I wanted to injure him, in any way available.

I asked my mother if we could go to the police and get them to warn Harvey off. But she replied that she did not think it would be considered a crime to tease dogs, and in any event she was nervous about going to the police for any reason whatsoever.

Then, unexpectedly, Harvey played into our hands.

I owned a telescope which had once belonged to a MacLeod ancestor who had been in the Royal Navy. It was brass, and it pulled out to three lengths, the largest segment being encased in dark leather interestingly scratched and scuffed with the marks of who-knows-what sea battles or forays into dangerous waters. The lenses were still in perfect condition, and if you sat up in one of our spruce trees you could see every detail of houses two blocks away. I was too old now to climb trees and spy, but my brother often did. One day I found him waiting for me on the front porch.

"Vanessa—" he blurted, "the telescope's gone."

"If you've lost it, Roddie MacLeod, I'll—"

"I never!" he cried. "I left it on the grass near the gate, just for a minute, while I went in to get my rope so I could climb up. Harvey took it. Honest, Vanessa. I was just coming out the front door when I saw him ride off. And when I looked, the telescope was gone."

"Listen, Roddie, you didn't actually see him pick it up?"

"No, but who else could it have been?"

"Did you look carefully for it?"

"Sure, I did," he said indignantly. "Go ahead—look yourself."

I looked, but the telescope wasn't anywhere on the lawn. This time I did not hesitate about telling my mother. This was too good an opportunity to miss. I felt jubilant and excited. I felt like shouting some Highland war-cry, or perhaps whistling *The Mac-Leod's Praise*. Or quoting some embattled line from Holy Writ. Vengeance is mine, saith the Lord.

"In a way, it's kind of peculiar," I said to my mother, talking so rapidly she could hardly make out what I was saying. "You know, like getting Al Capone on income-tax evasion instead of murder."

"Stop dramatising everything, Vanessa," my mother said, "and let me think for a minute what would be the best thing to do."

"What's all this?" Grandfather Connor demanded crossly, having been roused from his chair by the tumult of my voice.

My mother told him, and he was in no doubt what to do.

"Get your coat on, Vanessa. We're going over there right now."

I looked at him, stunned. Then I shook my head firmly.

"It's a matter for the police."

"Rubbish," my grandfather snapped, unable to acknowledge any authority except his own. "What could Rufus Nolan do that I can't do? He's a fool of a man anyway."

I had not bargained on this. I was out for blood, but I would have preferred someone else to draw it.

"You go then," I said sullenly. "I don't want to."

"You'd better go with him, Vanessa," my mother said. "Father wouldn't recognise the telescope. He's never had anything to do with it."

"I don't know where Harvey lives," I stalled.

"I know where he lives," my grandfather said. "It's Ada Shinwell's house, at the North End, right beside the C.P.R. tracks. Vanessa, for the last time, you get your coat on and come along."

I got my coat on and came along. The North End of Manawaka was full of shacks and shanties, unpainted boards, roofs with half the shingles missing, windows with limp hole-spattered lace curtains or else no curtains at all, chickens milling moronically in yards where the fences had never been lifted when they leaned and the weeds never hacked at or fought down. The cement sidewalks were broken, great chunks heaved up by frost and never repaired, for the Town Council did not pay much attention to this part of town. A few scraggy structures had once been stores but had been deserted when some of the town prospered and moved south, away from the tracks. Now the old signs could still be seen, weathered to peeling pastels, grimy pink that had once shouted crimsonly "Barnes' Grain and Feed," and a mute rotting green that had once boldly been "Thurson's General Store." The windows of these ex-shops were boarded over now, and they were used only as warehouses or roofs over the heads of rodents and tramps.

At the furthest point of the town the C.P.R. station stood, respectably painted in the gloomy maroon colour known as Railway Red, paradoxically neat in the midst of the decrepit buildings around it. Above and beyond the station rose the peaked roofs of the grain elevators, solid and ugly but the closest thing there was to towers here.

I knew Harvey had been brought up by his aunt, his dead mother's sister, but that was all I knew about him. My grandfather went directly to the place. It was a small square frame house with wooden lace along the front porch. At one time it must have been white, but it had not been painted for years. The rust-corroded gate stood open and askew, having apparently once been wrenched off its hinges. In the yard the goldenrod grew, and the tall uncut grass had formed seed-nodules like oats. My grandfather knocked at the door.

"Yes?"

The woman was big and haggard, and her face, wrinkled like elm bark, was spread thickly with a mauvish powder. Her grey hair was snipped short like a man's. She wore a brown tweed skirt which looked as though it had never been cleaned throughout a long life, and a tight-fitting and filthy peach-coloured sweater that betrayed her gaunt and plank-flat body.

"Well, if it ain't Mr. Connor," she said sarcastically.

"Where's your boy, Ada?" my grandfather demanded.

"What's he done?" she asked immediately.

"Stole a telescope. I want it back."

The door opened wider.

"Come in," Harvey's aunt said.

The house was not divided into living room and kitchen. There was one large room on the ground floor and it was used for everything. At one end the black wooden stove stood surrounded by pots and pans hanging on nails from the wall. The table was covered with oilcloth, the worn-off pattern showing only feebly. The dishes from breakfast were still there, the grease stiffened on them, the puddles of egg yolk turned to yellow glue. On the cabinet stood a brown crockery basin with a wooden spoon and batter in it— the pancakes for tonight's meal. The house had that acrid sour-milk and ammonia smell that comes from food left lying around and chamber pots full of urine unemptied until they are overflowing.

In the front part of the room stood two armchairs with the plum velour ripped and stained, and a spineless sofa, sagging in the middle, once blue plush and now grimed to a grey calico. On the sofa sat Harvey. His long legs were thrust forward and his head lolled to one side. He looked as though he were pretending, without much acting ability, to be asleep.

His aunt darted in like a giant darning needle.

"All right, you. Where is it?"

It seemed strange that she would ask him this question straightaway. She never asked him whether or not he had actually taken it.

Harvey did not reply. He lay there on the sofa, his eyes flickering open, then half closing again. His aunt, with an explosive quickness that made me jerk in every nerve, snatched the wooden spoon out of the bowl of batter and hit him across the face.

Harvey's eyes opened a little more, but only a little. The amber slits stared at her, but he did not move. He bore it, that she had hit him like that, and in front of other people. He was not a kid any longer. His shoulders and body looked immensely strong. He could have thrust her hand away, or held her wrists.

He could have walked out. But he had not done so. Slowly, with a clown's grin, he wiped the batter off his face.

"All right," she said. "I'll give you one chance more, and that's all. After that, you know what."

I never discovered what final card she held. Would she have turned him over to the Mounties, or thrown him out of the house? It did not really matter. Maybe the threat was one left over from childhood, still believed in by both of them, out of habit. Or maybe there was no specific threat at all, only a matter of one will being able to inflict what it chose upon another.

He lumbered to his feet, and in a few minutes he came back to the room. He threw the telescope on the floor, and he gave me a devastatingly scornful look. Then he sat down on the sofa once more.

His aunt picked up the telescope and handed it to my grandfather. Her voice was a whine, but underneath it there was a desolate anger.

"You're not gonna go to the police, are you? Listen, you got no idea how it's been. What was I supposed to do, left with a kid to look after? Who'd have married me? What man would've taken on that? He's never been anything but trouble to me. Who do you think he takes after? Some shit nobody but her ever seen."

"I'm not going to the police," my grandfather said aloofly. Then he went away.

"Did you know her, before?" I asked him, when we were walking home.

"No," my grandfather replied without interest. "She was nobody a person would know, to speak of. She was just always around town, that's all."

Harvey's pestering of Nanuk stopped, for soon afterwards he quit school, dropped the paper route, and got a job with Yang Min, the elderly Chinese who kept a small café at the North End, where the railway section hands went for coffee.

For Nanuk, the respite came too late. He had become increasingly suspicious of everyone except the family, and anyone who approached the front gate when he was in the yard was met in the same way, with the low warning growl. If they attempted to open the gate, he would stand there, poised and bristling, waiting for their next move. Their next move became predictable. Whoever it happened to be would quietly close the gate and go away. They would then phone my mother. Sometimes Grandfather Connor would answer the phone. They would tell him about Nanuk, and he would rant at my mother for the rest of the day, saying that all Huskies were savage by nature.

"Listen, Vanessa, I want to talk to you," my mother said. "Grandfather knows someone on a farm out by Freehold who's willing to take Nanuk. It would be a much better place for him. He could run around. And on a farm, he wouldn't be so much of a danger."

I knew there was no point in arguing. It had become inevitable. Nanuk was taken away on a morning when I was at school. I did not say goodbye to him. I did not want to. I mourned for him secretly, but after a while I no longer thought about him so very much.

About a year later, the Starlite Café at the North End was robbed. Yang Min, the old man who owned it, was found unconscious on the floor. He had been badly beaten up.

They caught Harvey quite quickly. He had hopped a freight. The Mounties picked him up only two stops beyond Manawaka.

"Apparently he didn't even try to deny it," my mother said. "Not that it would've done him much good. You'd have thought he would have hidden the money, though, wouldn't you?"

What I said then surprised me as much as it did

my mother. I had not known I was going to ask this question. I had not known it was there to be asked.

"Mother—what really happened to Nanuk?"

My mother looked shocked and distressed.

"What makes you think—?"

"Never mind," I said. "Just tell me."

Her voice was almost inaudible, and there was a resignation in it, as though she had given up trying to make everything all right.

"The vet took him," she said, "and chloroformed him. Well, what else could I do, Vanessa? He wasn't safe to go free."

Harvey Shinwell got six years. I never saw him again. I don't know where he went when he got out. Back in, I suppose.

I used to see his aunt occasionally on the street. She was considered safe to go free. Once she said hello to me. I did not reply, although I knew that this was probably not fair, either.

Jericho's Brick Battlements

Before we moved into it, the Brick House had always been a Sunday place to me. It was a fine place for visiting. To live there, however, was unthinkable. This would probably never have been necessary, if my father had not died suddenly that winter. That spring, with the wind only beginning to thaw and the roads flowing muddily with melted snow, my mother had told me that she and my brother and myself would be going to the Brick House to live.

"You're twelve and a half, Vanessa," she had pointed out, unnecessarily and almost defensively, as though she anticipated my protests. "That's quite old enough to understand. We can't afford to keep two houses going, and there are Grandfather and Aunt Edna rattling around down there all by themselves."

"I don't want to go," I said, knowing it was making her feel worse than she already did, but unable to stop myself. "I don't want to live there. Not with *him*."

"He's my father, Vanessa," she said, dredging up the words as though they belonged to her duty self rather than her own self, "and he's your grandfather, so you will please kindly not speak that way about him."

The day we moved, I watched the man carry in the crates and barrels which held the MacLeod silver and china, and the trunks and cardboard boxes which held our clothes and assorted possessions. Nearly all the furniture had been sold. I wanted the movers to walk slowly, dragging their feet, but they lugged the boxes briskly, joking as though nothing were the matter. I spotted among the other things the suitcase which contained my own treasured objects—a blue glass slipper like Cinderella's, a shiny wooden darning egg, which had been brought from Scotland ages ago and which bore a picture of a town so miniature that you had to use a magnifying glass to see the streets and name—"Helensburgh, on the Clyde," a dozen or so unmatched dangling bead earrings discarded by Aunt Edna, a white silk bookmark which said "Feed My Sheep," in cross-stitch, and the leather-bound telescope which some distant naval MacLeod had once used to sight the enemy. There was a kind of finality about seeing this suitcase of mine going the way of all the other boxes, up the front steps, across the verandah, through the front door of the Brick House. There could be no reversal of decisions now. I felt as though nothing favourable would ever be likely to happen again.

Grandfather Connor, dressed in his huge and rank-smelling bear coat despite the mild air, was directing traffic from the top step.

"Mind how you take them barrels in," he warned. "The plate glass in that door cost me something, I can tell you, and I'll not have you crashing into it. Easy, man—can't you see where you're going? You're not getting paid to walk around with your eyes shut. That's it—straight through the front hall, now and into the kitchen."

He caught sight of me, lurking beside the caragana hedge.

"Come on, Vanessa," he shouted. "A big girl like you—can't you even give your mother a hand? I can't abide people standing around doing nothing. If you're this bone-idle now, the Lord only knows what you'll grow up to be like. Come on, now!"

In the kitchen, which was sweltering from the heat of the black woodstove big enough to cook for a threshing gang, my mother and aunt were unpacking while my brother, who was not quite three, was

delightedly shuffling through the offcast bits of newspaper which lay like piles of autumn leaves on the
floor. My grandfather had followed me in. He looked
at the plates and cups and soup tureens which were
emerging from one of the barrels as my mother pulled
off the newspaper and set the china on the floor.

"I don't know why you're unpacking all that stuff,
Beth," Grandfather Connor remarked. "It'll just have
to go back in again."

My mother looked up in surprise.

"It's the MacLeod china," she said. "It's Limoges.
I thought we'd use it."

"We've got no room for it here," my grandfather said decidedly. "It'll have to go in the basement."

"But Father—"

"No buts about it," Grandfather Connor inter-
rupted. "We don't need no china of the MacLeods.
We got plenty of our own. I'm not having it up here."

My mother looked at the plate she was holding. It
was edged in gold and it had tiny moss roses on it.
She shrugged and began wrapping it up in the newspaper once more. When my grandfather had gone
outside once more to supervise the movers, Aunt Edna
turned to my mother.

"For mercy's sake, Beth, why didn't you say we'd
be keeping it out and he could just lump it?"

"What's the use?" my mother replied. "It's like
batting your head against a brick wall. He'd get his
way in the end. He always does. How you can keep on
arguing, Edna, after all this time, I just don't know. It
would play me out."

"Well, if you're going to make a carpet of yourself," my aunt said aggressively, "he'll sure as death
walk all over you. Look at the way he was with Mother."

"I don't know," my mother said. "She never met
him head-on like you do, but I'll bet she got on better
that way. Look at this, Edna. It's the barrel with the

silver. Here we are with two entire silver tea services, Mother's and the MacLeods', and hardly a nickel to our names. I suppose it's funny in a way."

"Funny peculiar," my aunt commented. "Not funny ha ha."

"What on earth are we going to do with it all?" my mother enquired.

"Sell it," my aunt suggested tersely, "and buy a case of rye."

I went out into the back yard. The old stable at the end of the garden was locked, but I had long ago discovered a way in. A flimsy outside staircase led up to the loft, which was never locked, for it contained only empty boxes and sparrows' nests and a few broken chairs. I went up, found the two loose boards, lifted them and lowered myself down to the stable rafters below. From there it was an easy jump to the roof of the MacLaughlin-Buick and down to the ground.

Grandfather Connor's car, the only one he ever owned, had not been driven for years now, but he refused to part with it. It had tall thin wheels and the body of it was high and square. The seats were beige and brown-striped plush, and they looked nearly as unworn now as they must have done when the car was new, long before I was born. He had never driven it very much and had always taken great care of it. Perhaps he had thought it was too expensive to be used except occasionally. Or perhaps he had never grown accustomed to the fact that it could not be controlled by shouting.

I opened the door of the car and climbed inside. I did not think Grandfather Connor or anyone else ever came here any more. Now I was glad I had never told anyone about the loose boards in the loft. There were black oilcloth side-pockets inside the car doors. They would do nicely to keep scribblers and pencils in. I lay back on the striped plush and propped my feet devilishly against a window, not caring if I scraped the glass or scratched the paintwork. I began to size up the inner situation, which was a relief from the outer. I already had half a five-cent scribbler full of the story I was writing.

The tale was set in Quebec in the early days of the fur trade. The heroine's name was Marie. It had to be a tossup between Marie and Antoinette, owing to a somewhat limited choice on my part, and I had finally rejected Antoinette as being too fancy. Orphaned young, Marie was forced to work at the Inn of the Grey Cat. *La Chat? Le Chat?* And what was Grey? They didn't teach French until high school in Manawaka, and I wasn't there yet. But never mind. These were trivial details. The main thing was that Marie had overheard the stealthy conversation of two handsome although shabbily dressed *voyageurs,* who later would turn out to be the great *coureurs-de-bois,* Radisson and Groseilliers. The problem was now plain. How to get Marie out of her unpromising life at the inn and onto the ship which would carry her to France? And once in France, then what? Neither Radisson nor Groseilliers would marry her, I was pretty sure of that. They were both too busy with changing back and forth from the side of the French to the side of the English, and besides, they were too old for her.

I lay on the seat of the MacLaughlin-Buick feeling disenchantment begin to set in. Marie would not get out of the grey stone inn. She would stay there all her life. The only thing that would ever happen to her was that she would get older. Probably the *voyageurs* weren't Radisson and Groseilliers at all. Or if they were, they wouldn't give her a second glance. I felt I could not bear it. I no longer wanted to finish the story. What was the use, if she couldn't get out except by ruses which clearly wouldn't happen in real life?

I climbed over into the front seat of the car and sat for a moment with my hands on the stiff black steering wheel. There, in the middle, was the button which used to make the horn work. All at once I could hear that horn again, loudly, in my head, and I remembered something I didn't know I knew. I remembered riding in the MacLaughlin-Buick with my grandfather. It was a memory with nothing around it, an unplaced memory without geography or time. I must have been exceedingly young, four at most. I was sitting small and low on the front seat, hardly high enough to see out through the windscreen. My grandfather was sitting straight and haughty behind the steering wheel. And the car was flying, flying, flying, through the widespread streets of that enormous town, and its horn was bannering our presence as we conquered. *A-hoo-gah! A-hoo-gah!* I was gazing with love and glory at my giant grandfather as he drove his valiant chariot through all the streets of this world.

I closed the car door carefully. Then I climbed to the rafters and hauled myself back up into the loft. I looked around and discovered a packingcase that would do for a desk. A scribbler could be hidden in a dozen places. The loft was easier to get at. There was more space here, really. It would be a better place to be mine than the garage below.

When I had turned fourteen, the new C.N.R. stationmaster, Wes Grigg, began to visit the Brick House. He came to see Aunt Edna. She had had admirers before, but not for some time now. In the old days, or what I regarded as the old days, when she used to work as a secretary in Winnipeg, she had been—according to my mother—popular but too flippant. The prospects in Manawaka were far from numerous and had not increased over the years. Apart from Stanley Urquhart who worked at Donatello's Barbershop and who exuded repugnantly the blended odours of bay rum and Dentyne chewing gun, or Cluny MacPherson from the B.A. Garage who was about five feet tall, Manawaka was singularly lacking in unattached men of a suitable age. Men either married young and resigned themselves, or they left town and who could blame them? Aunt Edna's life, since she came back, had not exactly been filled with gaiety. She hardly ever went out in the evenings, except occasionally to a movie with mother. To external view she remained her old wisecracking self. When life in the Brick House was really getting her down, she would work off steam on the piano.

"C'mon, kiddo," she would say, especially on days when Grandfather Connor had been remarking that he couldn't for the life of him see why she didn't get a man for herself and get married like every other decent woman, "what about a little something to soothe the savage breast, eh?"

She would plunk herself down on the piano bench, push up her sweater sleeves, and crash into "The Twelfth Street Rag." The notes would jitter and prance, strut defiantly, swagger from ceiling to floor and out the window, making my feet want to follow them, away off somewhere, far away from home, where the swinging shoes winged continually in dawns beyond our dimensions. "Tiger Rag." "Bye Bye Blackbird." She would be playing so loudly that we never heard Grandfather Connor's arrival.

"I don't know why you waste your time on that rubbish, Edna," he would say, for the only music he considered worthy of the name were hymn tunes and "God Save the King."

She would ignore him and keep on playing. He would sink heavily into his oak chair.

"A man can't hear hisself think," he would announce.

No response. She would begin pounding out "I Wish I Could Shimmy Like My Sister Kate."

"Edna, cut it out this second before I lose my patience!"

Only then would my aunt stop. She would wink at me, maybe even laugh, but she would stop.

"Lose his patience indeed," she would mutter as we went into the kitchen. "Kindly inform me when he ever found it."

Aunt Edna was nearly thirty-three when Wes Grigg came to Manawaka. She did not seem to have changed much in appearance from my earliest memories of her. She had taken to having her straight black hair permed instead of bobbed, that was all, and her tall rangy figure was most often clad in a skirt and sweater now, instead of the smart tailored suits in paddy-green or lilac which she used to wear. Wes was taller than Aunt Edna, and distinctly middle-aged. His thick shaggy hair was the colour my mother called "pepper and salt," black beginning to go grey. His eyebrows, too, were grey and thick and shaggy, and his herringbone tweed jacket was hairy as a horse blanket. He reminded me of the Shaggy Man in one of the *Oz* books. I did not mean this in any critical sense. It made me like him better. There was something solid and reassuring about him, and yet he was the reverse of stern. He was quiet-spoken and never argued, but he laughed a fair amount, especially at his own jokes, which were usually pretty corny, and he did his damnedest to please Aunt Edna.

Early one evening the doorbell dinged and it was Wes.

"I thought I'd drop around to see if you'd like to go to Winnipeg in a couple weeks' time, Edna," he said. "Just for the day, you know. Kester's promised to look after everything here. I got some time coming to me. We could get the morning train on a Thursday. How about it?"

"Mercy," my aunt said, stalling. "The bright lights would dazzle me. I haven't been that far in ages now. I didn't know you were rich."

Wes reddened.

"Well, I got my pass, you know. It wouldn't be that much for your ticket. We could see a show and have dinner, get the night train back. Anyways, what do you say?"

"Well—" my aunt said.

My mother and I, hovering in the hall like amateurish spies, gave one another a glance.

"I couldn't help overhearing," my mother carolled.

"You *go*, Edna. You haven't been away for I don't know *how* long. Go on. Go ahead."

"Well—" my aunt said again. "Well, I guess so, Wes. Thanks. I mean, it's very nice of you."

"You might as well stay for supper, Wes, now that you're here," my mother added.

"Oh—well, thanks, Beth, if you're sure it's okay."

"Certainly, certainly," my mother assured him, and flew out to the kitchen, to change her mind about supper, which was to have been scrambled eggs on toast but was almost instantly turned into pancakes and maple syrup.

Aunt Edna talked in a desultory fashion to Wes for a few minutes and then left him in the living room. Grandfather Connor, who had been dozing in his chair, now became alert. His ice-blue eyes, still as penetrating as they had ever been, focussed sharply on Wes.

"Who're you?" he demanded.

It did not seem a very auspicious beginning for a conversation. I hung around in the hall to listen, and when my brother Roddie came running down the front stairs and began to talk to me, I shushed him rapidly and shooed him into the kitchen.

"Grigg's the name," Wes said. "Wes Grigg. You remember me, Mr. Connor. I been here before."

Was it possible—oh joy—that Grandfather was losing his memory? Would he no longer be able to muster up at a moment's notice every past misdemeanor of mine? On the other hand, it could have awkward consequences, as now.

"Let me get a good look at you," Grandfather was saying. "I seen you before—yes. What're you doing here? Come to see Edna?"

"Well, yes."

"We're just going to have our supper," Grandfather Connor said, taking his gold watch out of his vest pocket. "You'd best not stay long. We're just going to have our supper. If we ever get it. It's away past six."

I looked at my own watch. It was three minutes past six.

"Well—Beth's kindly asked me to stay," Wes mumbled.

"What?" Grandfather Connor demanded, exaggerating his deafness as he quite often did for purposes of confounding the person to whom he was talking. Nothing makes you feel more like a moron than being required to repeat an uninspired sentence four times.

"I said—Beth's kindly asked me to stay," Wes said distinctly.

"Stay? Stay here? What for? What's the woman thinking of?"

"No—to stay for supper," Wes bellowed agonisedly.

"Oh," Grandfather Connor said flatly. "Well, if she wants to feed the whole neighbourhood, that's her lookout. Don't know who she thinks pays the grocery bills, though."

Enough was enough. I ploughed into the living room and stared at Grandfather. I did not speak. I only stared my anger, and he stared his right back. Finally I turned away.

"Hi, Wes," I said. "Gee—what a night, eh? Think we'll have a blizzard?"

It was February, and the wind outside sounded like the shrill hooting of demons in an ice hell. It slapped and battered against the walls of the Brick House until it seemed as though the storm windows could not hold, although I knew they would.

"Yeh, it's terrible all right," Wes agreed, "but I dunno, Vanessa—the forecast's not for a blizzard."

"Them weather men are always wrong," my grandfather put in.

"No, they're not," I contradicted vehemently, as though the principle involved were one concerning my very soul's honour. "They're usually perfectly right. Well, they are *so*. They forecast that storm in January and we got it all right, didn't we?"

"They can't tell no more than what I can with

that old barometer up in the verandah there," my grandfather replied, undaunted.

I left the field temporarily and skimmed out to the kitchen to get a picture of the situation there. My mother was ladling pancake batter onto the black iron frying pan. My aunt was opening a jar of peaches, and on her face was a look of annoyance.

"Honestly, Beth," she was saying, "I know you mean well, honey, but you don't have to absolutely *throw* me at the poor guy."

"I wasn't throwing anybody at anybody," my mother answered placidly, something in her voice reminding me of the way Grandmother Connor used to speak, gently but with certainty. "I merely asked him to stay to supper, that's all. If you can't ask a person to stay to supper on a night like this, there must be something wrong with you. And I just can't see why you didn't agree right away to go to Winnipeg, Edna. Personally, I thought it was nice of Wes. Very nice, in fact."

My aunt looked up from the peaches with a quizzical expression.

"Well, it was because I had a kind of notion that he was going to—"

"Going to what?" my mother enquired. "Ask you to stay overnight? So what? Really, Edna, if you were sixteen you might be upset, but *really*—"

My aunt burst out laughing.

"Beth, don't be idiotic! I didn't mean that. I only meant I thought he might ask me to marry him. I could, of course, be wrong. Edna Connor has never been widely known for her infallibility."

"For Pete's sake," my mother said in exasperation, "what's so worrying about it if he does? All you have to say is either Yes or No."

"Very simple," my aunt said gloomily, "I don't think."

"He's kind," my mother ventured.

"That's true," my aunt agreed. "I wish he didn't say *somewheres*, though."

"Don't be silly," my mother said. "What does it matter? He's got a regular job."

"I know it, Beth. But did you know he is a Baptist?"

"So was Mother. There's nothing wrong with being a Baptist."

"I'm not religious," my aunt pointed out.

"Well, you wouldn't have to go. He's not an unreasonable man."

"I know he's not. But did you know he's got an ulcer and there's all kinds of things he can't eat?"

"I don't believe it would kill you if you never ate roast pork again as long as you live," my adamant mother replied.

"Beth—just don't propagandise me," my aunt pleaded.

My mother looked stricken and remorseful.

"Oh honey, I didn't mean it to sound that way. Honestly, I didn't. It's just that you've been keeping house for Father all this time, and you've had so little life of your own. It's just that it would be wonderful if you could get *out*."

"What about you?" Aunt Edna said. "How are you going to get out?"

"It's different for me," my mother replied in a low voice. "I've had those years with Ewen. I have Vanessa and Roddie. Maybe I can't get out. But they will."

There was a silence. Neither of them had noticed me standing in the doorway. I felt as though I ought to vanish, as though I had been intruding on a totally private matter.

"I'm not trying to push you in the slightest," my mother said. "But you know how much you've wanted to go."

"Yes," Aunt Edna said. "But now it comes to it—I don't know. And I'm fond of Wes. That's the odd part. I really am fond of him. It sounds funny coming from me, I guess, but he's—well, he's a good man, Beth."

"It doesn't sound funny at all. I know he is."

My aunt all at once resumed her usual voice.

"And you don't need to tell me what the song says, either. A good man nowadays is hard to find."

"Edna—" my mother said anxiously. "What's the matter? What's troubling you?"

"I don't know," Aunt Edna hesitated. "I guess I've got used to being back here in the old dungeon. It's strange, Beth. Father's impossible, and certainly no one has said it oftener than I have. I have less patience with him than any of us has ever had, except possibly Vanessa, and she's only fourteen, for Heaven's sake. I know all that. But, he's—well, I guess it's just that I have the feeling that the *absolute* worst wouldn't happen here, ever. Things wouldn't actually fall apart. Do you know what I mean? We got through the Depression somehow. We never thought we would, but we did. I know it's more by good luck than good management. I'm perfectly aware of all that. And yet—"

I backed quietly from the kitchen doorway into the dining room. I sensed that they would not really mind my overhearing as they once would have done. But I wished I had not heard, all the same.

Five minutes later Grandfather Connor's thumping footsteps approached the kitchen.

"Beth! Are you planning on having supper tonight or tomorrow morning?"

"It's coming right away," my mother replied, unruffled.

"You'd best speak to that Grigg, Edna," he went on, his voice loud enough to be heard in South Wachakwa, never mind our living room. "You better tell him he's not to turn up just at supper-time. Don't he have no food of his own? What'd he do for meals before he started coming here?"

"He's been here about five times, Father," Aunt Edna said. "And that is all. Good glory, can't you—"

"Supper!" my mother called. "All ready now."

After supper, when Roddie had been put to bed, my mother announced pointedly that she had some book catalogues to look through for the local library, so she thought she would just go upstairs for a while and do that. I followed her example by going up to my room to do my homework. Grandfather Connor, however, had no intention of leaving Wes and Aunt Edna alone, nor scarcely even allowing them a word in edgewise. The gist of Grandfather's theme tonight, from the portions of it that penetrated upstairs, seemed to be that the C.N.R. was losing all the taxpayers' money because any business the government had a hand in was bound to be inferior and if Wes had any brains he'd be working for the C.P.R. instead. At that point Wes must have been foolish enough to mention the proposed jaunt to Winnipeg, for I heard Grandfather's explosive voice.

"*Winnipeg!* You'll do no such thing, Edna. I'll not have you going there with *him!*"

Winnipeg sounded like Sodom and Gomorrah, and Wes like a combination of Casanova and the Marquis de Sade.

"I'm going," Aunt Edna said. "It's only for one day."

"Only for the *day!*" Grandfather Connor roared, making it apparent that they were not to deceive themselves into thinking he was one of those who believe illicit love can take place only after dark.

"This is ridiculous!" Aunt Edna snapped. "Father, can't you please, just for once—"

"Ridiculous, is it?" Grandfather Connor asked dramatically. "Ridiculous, eh? Well, let it be ridiculous, then. You're not going. That's all."

I heard his footsteps descending the basement stairs. He would sit in his familiar rocking chair beside the furnace. That chair must have been the most vocal one in the whole world. Perhaps something was eccentric about its timbers, or perhaps its maker had designed it to produce that *screee-scraaaw* at the slightest movement of its rockers. As usual Grandfather would now register his state of mind unmistakably until he heard Wes leave the house. Aunt

Edna, on her way up to the bathroom, poked her head into my bedroom.

"You know something, kiddo? The rocking chair business has gone on so long now that I hardly even find it embarrassing any more. Remember that, in a few years' time, eh?"

"Why?"

"Because," Aunt Edna said, and although she was smiling, neither of us took it as a joke, "it'll be your turn then."

Half an hour later, the pipes caught fire. Excitement was never in vast supply at the Brick House, but that was one kind of excitement we could have done without. The wood furnace was old but sound, and in the coldest weather my grandfather would stoke it up high with his special mixture of birch and poplar. It took a lot of fire to keep the big house warm in winter. Upstairs, the pipes which led from the furnace were exposed and beginning to be fragile. My mother and aunt worried about them incessantly from November to April. My grandfather, who considered himself an expert in these matters, since he had spent years in running a hardware business which sold such pipes among other things, maintained they were perfectly safe, and Beth and Edna were fretting over nothing. I was finishing my homework when I became aware of a smell like scorched paint.

In my grandfather's room the pipe was a bright light crimson. From inside its dragon throat came a low but impressive rumble. I yelled at the top of my voice.

"The pipes are on fire! Quick!"

My grandfather pounded up from the basement, then down again, then up again, proclaiming that the pipes would soon simmer down and everyone was to stop fussing this minute. My mother screamed, "Roddie!" and went in to wake and dress him in his snowsuit just in case, and he, understandably agitated at being pounced upon and muffled up in his winter toggery in what must have seemed the middle of the night, sobbed gustily. Aunt Edna kept screeching that someone positively must phone the fire brigade, but my grandfather refused even to consider the idea. What, he demanded with more force than logic, could the fire brigade do that he couldn't do? Aunt Edna replied that if he wanted his own house burned down around his ears that was his concern and personally she wouldn't shed a tear. I went back to my room, filled two pillowcases with precious possessions of one sort and another, put on two of my heaviest sweaters and steadied myself to flee into the night.

The pipes were gurgling redly.

"Hey! Where's Wes?" I asked.

"Gone to fetch someone or something," Aunt Edna replied distractedly. "I hope to Heaven he hurries. Just *listen* to them, Vanessa. Do you think you could keep Father here while I slip down and phone the fire brigade?"

"No," I said, "but I think you ought to do it anyway. We're going to feel pretty silly if the house really does catch fire and we have to say we never even tried to stop it."

"You're darned right we are," Aunt Edna agreed.

"Well, I don't know, Edna," my mother vacillated, still clutching Roddie, who was still howling. "We've had this with the pipes before and they've never actually—"

The pipes were beginning to chortle evilly. The light crimson was getting lighter and presumably hotter. The stench was terrible.

Just then the front door opened and slammed shut again.

"Wes! Where on earth have you *been*?" my aunt cried.

"I went to get some stuff we use at the station

when this kinda thing happens," he explained. "Lucky my old car started first time."

"You're not going down there," Grandfather Connor said belligerently at the head of the basement stairs. The basement was his territory and his alone.

Wes pushed him aside, courteously but unarguably.

"Don't worry, Mr. Connor," he said, almost jovially. "If I damage your furnace you can always sue me."

We trooped down into the basement after him. Despite my grandfather's warnings and imprecations, Wes opened the furnace door and threw in a small boxful of blackish powder. For an instant I half expected the whole house to go up in a last mad explosion. But no. The magic powder acted swiftly. Where had it been all our lives? I could see my mother making a mental note to obtain six dozen boxes of it, whatever its cost, even if she had to pawn her pearl ring. The flame-roaring subsided. The voices of the pipes dwindled to a few chuffing wheezes and then fell silent.

"The man's a fool," my grandfather remarked to no one in particular. "If he'd left them pipes alone, they'd have done just the same. Can't for the life of me see why Edna wants to go and get herself mixed up with a fellow like that."

He was no doubt perfectly correct about the pipes. After all, it was not our first pipe fire, and the Brick House still stood. But the rest of us were not in any mood to believe him. My mother could see her worries receding to a thousand instead of a thousand and one.

"Now, now, Father," she said, beaming happily, "you've got to admit it did the trick. I wonder if you can buy that stuff in town or if you have to order it."

I could imagine her telling Aunt Edna how nice it was that Wes was so handy in a crisis. Personally, I thought it would cut a lot more ice with Aunt Edna if my mother reminded her of the way Wes had been with Grandfather Connor. But perhaps there was no need.

"Are you sure you honestly want to go to Winnipeg, Wes?" Aunt Edna was saying in the front hall. "I mean, I don't mind one way or another. It's up to you, I mean. It would be lovely to go, but it seems kind of a lot of money for us to go only for one day."

"I thought it might give me the nerve," Wes said. "Sometimes a different place'll do that. But now I come to think of it, maybe it would be better to go somewheres further, later on when the weather's better, and stay longer. I got eight days holidays coming to me, I didn't mention."

Nothing makes heroes of us like acts of heroism, even minor ones. His trouble was, as it turned out, that he had reached an age when he wasn't anxious to have his face slapped, metaphorically speaking. He had had the sneaking feeling that Aunt Edna was formidable. Little did he know that she was as unsure of herself in her way as he was in his. After the night of the pipe fire, he went out of his way to avoid argument with Grandfather. But none of us ever forgot. Aunt Edna, in a gesture which must have taken some doing, even learned to play "Jesus Calls Us O'er the Tumult," until she discovered with relief that Wes believed sufficient unto the Sabbath were the hymns thereof.

Wes and Aunt Edna were married in the spring, and she went to live at the C.N.R. station. After their honeymoon, that is, which they spent in distant Montreal, since she could travel on his railway pass now. I missed her, but I was glad she was gone and that she had a house of her own, even if she had to sleep to the sound of shunting boxcars. It was only a pity she had had to wait so long to go. I wondered how long I would have to wait.

I had gone out with boys on rare occasions, but I had never had what might be termed a boyfriend.

The boys who had taken me to a movie or walked me home after skating at the Manawaka Rink on a Saturday night were far from prepossessing. They were either shorter than I, or dandruff-ridden, or of a stunning stupidity. I was embarrassed at being seen with them, but I never turned down an invitation, for reasons of status. I would willingly have gone out with the village idiot, had there been one, rather than not go out at all. Mavis Duncan, my closest friend, was slender and short and had naturally wavy auburn hair. Anyone tall, washed, witty and handsome in the vicinity asked her out. I was five-foot seven and had naturally poker-straight black hair which I tortured excruciatingly and unsuccessfully into a limp pageboy style with aluminum rollers every night. I had decided early that I must do the best I could with what I had, which at that time did not seem to be much. During the war, when I was seventeen, the social situation in town altered beyond belief. The R.C.A.F. built an elementary training camp at South Wachakwa, only a few miles away, and on weekends Manawaka was miraculously descended upon by scores of airmen, for South Wachakwa had a school, a church and one store, and that was all. Manawaka, on the other hand, had the Flamingo Dance Hall, the beer parlour at the Queen Victoria Hotel, the Regal Café, and numerous high school girls, of whom I was one.

I used to go with Mavis Duncan and Stacey Cameron to the Saturday night dances at the Flamingo. All the girls would go this way, in groups of three or four, for moral support. The girls congregated at one side of the small slippery dance floor, and the boys jostled around at the other side. When the music began for each dance, Mavis and Stacey and I would be engaged in gay lighthearted chatter, with panicky hearts and queasy stomachs. What if no one asked us to dance? The girls who had not been asked usually whipped upstairs to the Powder Room and stayed there for as long as possible, applying and re-applying make-up, smoking, talking in our gay lighthearted fashion to other sufferers. But when we were asked to dance, despair melted like ice cubes in July, and we would go slithering and swooping across the floor in whomever's arms, suddenly fearless and lovely.

The music seemed the only music that ever was or ever would be. I had no means of knowing that it was being set into the mosaic of myself, and that it would pass away quickly and yet remain always as mine. "Chattanooga Choo-Choo." "Skylark." "I'll Be Seeing You." "I'm a Little on the Lonely Side." "Don't Get Around Much Any More."

It was at the Flamingo that I met Michael. He was twenty-three, taller than I, with sandy hair, and he had developed a mocking smile to camouflage his seriousness. He came from British Columbia, where he had worked in his father's lumber business before he joined up. He told me about the lumber camps, and I could see the donkey-engines and the high-riggers and the gigantic Douglas firs pluming and plummeting down like the fall of titans, out there in the ferned forests where the air was always cool blue and warm with sun, and where the black-spined trees stood close with the light lacing through.

"I'd like to take you there, Vanessa," Michael said.

He took me home to the Brick House instead, and kissed me, and told me he'd see me next weekend. After that, I saw him every time he could get to Manawaka. Sometimes he would manage to get over just for an hour or so in the evening, hitching a lift. In order to be alone we would walk down into the Wachakwa Valley, where the brown creek pelted shallowly over the stones, and the prairie poplars grew, their leaves now a translucent yellow with autumn. The grass was thick and high, and we could make a nest and lie there and hold one another. I never actually made love with him. I was afraid. He did not try to persuade me, although he knew I wanted to as much as he did. He accepted the fear which I could not accept myself, for I despised it but could not overcome it.

Like me, Michael wrote stories and poems, a fact which he did not divulge to his Air Force friends. When we were together, there was never enough time, for we had everything to talk about and discover. I tried not to remember that in a few months he would be going away. I had never met anyone before who was interested in the same things as I was. We read Stephen Spender's "I Think Continually of Those Who Were Truly Great."

The names of those who in their lives fought for life,
Who wore at their hearts the fire's centre.
Born of the sun they travelled a short while towards the
  sun,
And left the vivid air signed with their honour.

"It's one of my favourite poems," I said, "and yet it shouldn't be, maybe. There's something about it that isn't true, not for me, anyway."

"How do you mean, Nessa?"

"I don't know. It sounds fine to say you think continually of those who were truly great. But you don't. You forget them. Most of the time you don't think of them at all. That's the terrible thing. I guess I was thinking of Dieppe."

The war had not affected Manawaka very much until then. Most of the Manawaka boys had joined the Queen's Own Cameron Highlanders, and when the casualty lists came in from Dieppe, half the town's families were hit. MacDonald. Gunn. Kowalski. Macalister. Lobodiak. MacIntosh. Chorniuk. Kamchuk. MacPherson. All the Scots and Ukrainian names of the boys a couple of years older than I was, the boys I had known all my life. When it happened, I had remembered that my father's brother Roderick had been killed in the First World War. He, too, had been eighteen, like most of these. It was then that war took on its meaning for me, a meaning that would never change. It meant only that people without choice in the matter were broken and spilled, and nothing could ever take the place of them. But I did not think of them continually. Even at this relatively short distance, I already thought of them only from time to time. It was this that seemed a betrayal.

"I know," Michael said. "And they weren't truly great, either. They just happened to be there. Hardly any poetry that I've seen says it the way it really is. You know what I think? Writing's going to change a lot after the war. It did after the First War and it will even more after this one. There aren't any heroes any more."

"I don't believe there ever were," I said. "Not in that way. I could be wrong. Spender's talking about the Battle of Britain pilots, partly anyway, isn't he? Maybe they were different. Why would they be, though? They were just there, too, and before they knew it, there wasn't any way to get out. Like the clansmen at Culloden. Or Ulysses' spearmen. Maybe even Ulysses, if he ever existed."

Michael looked up at the sky, where even now the training planes were skimming around like far-off blue-bottle flies.

"I don't know whether you're wrong or not," he said. "I don't know how other guys feel. It isn't what you call a topic for conversation. I only know how I feel. Every damn time I go up in one of those little Tiger Moths I can't stop sweating. What an admission, eh? If I'm like that on training planes, what the hell will I be like on bombers?"

He turned to me then and I held him tightly. There was nothing I could say to him. Too much had been said already, but perhaps it had not harmed him to speak the words. All I could do was hold him and hope that the force of my love would get through to him and have some value. What I really wanted was to marry him before he went away, but I was not yet eighteen, and we both knew my mother would not give her consent for me to marry anyone at my

age. After the war seemed a time too distant and in-
definite to contemplate, a time that would never
arrive.

When Michael had a weekend pass he would
stay at the Brick House, sleeping in Aunt Edna's old
room. He got on well with my mother, and she always welcomed him and did her best to shield him
from Grandfather Connor. This was not always possible. At meals, my grandfather would make muttering remarks about people who freeloaded on other
people's food. The rocking chair trick was used fairly
often, and when my mother and Michael and I were
doing the dishes we would hear the reproachful
screee-scraaaw coming from Grandfather's cavern.

"Just like old times," I remarked one evening.
"Remember how he was with Aunt Edna?"

"Now, now, dear," my mother said, torn between
a desire to sympathise with me and a feeling that
family skeletons were never to be paraded in front of
outsiders. "Well, if you must know, I do remember—
who could ever forget it? But we mustn't forget that
he's an old man."

"Heck, he was never any different that I can
recall," I said.

"Well, just try," my mother said, and I was reminded, as I often was with her, of Grandmother
Connor, who could not bear scenes either.

That evening was different from other evenings
which Michael had spent in the Brick House. Roddie
was in bed, my mother was writing letters at the
mahogany desk in the dining room, and Michael
and I were sitting on the huge shell-shaped chesterfield in the living room. My grandfather emerged
from the basement, winding his watch with obvious
intent.

"Aren't you folks ever going to sleep?" he demanded. "You plan on sitting up all night, Vanessa?"

"It's only eleven," I countered. "That's not late."

"Not late, eh?" Grandfather Connor said. "You're
still going to school, you know. You need your rest.

These late hours won't do you no good. No good at all."

He glared at Michael, who edged a little away from me.

"If Mother doesn't mind, I don't see why you should," I said.

"Your mother's got no sense," Grandfather Connor declared.

I had argued away at my mother over every possible facet of our existence, but I did not recall any of this now.

"She's got plenty of sense," I cried furiously. "She's got a darned sight more than you've ever had!"

My grandfather looked at me with dangerous eyes, and all at once, I was afraid of what he might say.

"You ought to know better than run around with a fellow like this," he said, his voice even and distinct and full of cold rage. "I'll bet a nickel to a doughnut hole he's married. That's the sort of fellow you've picked up, Vanessa."

I jumped to my feet and faced him. Our anger met and clashed silently. Then I shouted at him, as though if I sounded all my trumpets loudly enough, his walls would quake and crumble.

"That's a lie! Don't you dare say anything like that ever again! I won't hear it! I won't!"

I ran upstairs to my room and locked the door. My mother went into the living room and quieted my grandfather somehow. I could hear her apologising to Michael, and I felt the enormity of the task she was having to try to deal with. Then Grandfather Connor came stamping upstairs to his bedroom, and I went down again.

"It's okay, Nessa," Michael said, putting an arm around me. "Don't worry. It's all right. It doesn't matter."

Nevertheless, the next time he had a weekend leave, he did not come to the Brick House. He did not write or phone that week, either.

"It's just the same as it used to be with Aunt Edna," I stormed to my mother. "Remember the men *he* drove away from her? Until Wes, nobody kept coming around for long."

"It wasn't really that way," my mother said. "A man isn't driven away that easily, Vanessa. Don't worry. Maybe Michael's got flu or something."

It was December by this time, and flu was rampant. I told myself this was the reason I hadn't heard from him. Then I got flu myself. I got it at the worst possible time, for there was a dance at the South Wachakwa camp, and two buses were taking girls from Manawaka, suitably chaperoned. Mavis would be going, and all the others, but not me. I coughed and felt nauseated and wept with self-pity.

The next day Mavis came to see me after school.

"Don't go too close, dear," I could hear my mother saying in the front hall. "She may still be infectious."

"Oh, it's okay, Mrs. MacLeod," Mavis said. "I'm not very susceptible."

She came up to my room and sat down on the chair beside my dressing-table. She did not look like herself. She looked anxious and—what?

"Mavis—what's the matter? How was the dance? Did you see Michael?"

"Yeh," she said. "I saw him, Nessa."

Then she told me.

Michael had been with a fairly pretty brunette with a fancy hair-do. When Mavis said *Hi* to him, the girl asked to be introduced, and then she introduced herself. She was Michael's wife. She had come from Vancouver to visit him, a surprise visit. Michael's parents had paid her train fare. She couldn't stay at the camp, so she was staying at the Queen Victoria Hotel in Manawaka for a week. Michael was getting over as often as he could, which wasn't half often enough, she had said, laughing. He seemed to have to sneak in and out of Manawaka like a criminal, she had said, and wasn't the Air Force crazy? Mavis had replied yes, very crazy, and had walked away.

"Nessa—I'm sorry," Mavis said. "I mean it."

I believed her. We had known each other all our lives, she and I, and from grade one onwards we had often quarrelled and been rivals in every way. But we cared about one another. She really was sorry. If there had been anything she could have done to help, she would have done it. But there was nothing.

I did not tell my mother what had happened. From my general demeanor and from the disappearance of Michael she gathered enough.

"Vanessa," she said hesitantly one day, "I know you won't believe me, honey, but after a while it won't hurt so much. And yet in a way I guess it always will, to some extent. There doesn't seem to be anything anybody can do about that."

As it happened, she was right on all counts. I did not at the time believe her. But after a while it did not hurt so much. And yet twenty years later it was still with me to some extent, part of the accumulation of happenings which can never entirely be thrown away.

In those months that followed, I hated my grandfather as I had never hated him before. What I could not forgive was that he had been right, unwittingly right, for I did not believe for one moment that he had really thought Michael was married.

I was frantic to get away from Manawaka and from the Brick House, but I did not see how it was going to be possible. To take a business course would not have been too expensive, but I thought I would make a rotten secretary. When I applied to the women's Air Force, they told me they had enough recruits and advised me to continue my education. How? On what money? When I had finished high school, however, my mother told me that I would be able to go to university after all.

"Now don't fuss about it, Nessa," she said, "and

for mercy's sake let us not have any false pride. I've gone to Patrick Irwin at the jewellery store and he says the MacLeod silver and Limoges will fetch about three hundred dollars."

"I won't," I said. "It's not right. I can't."

"Oh yes you can," my mother said blithely, "and you will. For my sake, if nothing else. Do you think I want you to stay here for ever? Please don't be stubborn, honey. Also, Wes and Aunt Edna can contribute something, and so can your Aunt Florence and Uncle Terence."

"What have you done?" I cried. "Canvassed the entire family?"

"More or less," my mother said calmly, as though the tigress beneath her exterior was nothing to be surprised about. "Father is also selling some bonds which he's been hanging onto all these years."

"Him! How did you do that? But I'm not taking a nickel of his money."

My mother put a hand on my shoulder.

"When I was your age," she said, "I got the highest marks in the province in my last year of high school. I guess I never told you that. I wanted to go to college. Your grandfather didn't believe in education for women, then."

So I went. The day I left for Winnipeg, Wes and Aunt Edna drove me to the bus station. My mother did not come along. She said she would rather say goodbye to me at home. She and my brother stood on the front steps and waved as Wes started the car. I waved back. Now I was really going. And yet in some way which I could not define or understand, I did not feel nearly as free as I had expected to feel.

Two years later, when I was beginning my third year at university, I got an abrupt phone call from Manawaka.

"Vanessa?" my mother's voice, distant and close, came over the crackling wires. "Listen, honey, can you come home? It's Father. He's had a stroke."

I got the first bus back to Manawaka. By the time I arrived, he was dead. He had lived nearly ninety-four years.

My grandfather's funeral was the first I had ever attended. When Grandmother Connor died and when my father died, I had been too young. This time I had to go. I was twenty. I could no longer expect to be protected from the bizarre cruelty of such rituals.

Before the funeral, I kept thinking oddly of the time when my Great-Uncle Dan died. I hadn't attended that funeral, either, but it was one I wouldn't have minded going to. Dan had never ceased being a no-good, a natural-born stage Irishman, who continued even when he was senile to sing rebel songs. For years Grandfather Connor had virtually supported him. His funeral must have been quiet and impoverished, but in my head I had always imagined the funeral he ought to have had. His coffin should have been borne by a hayrack festooned with green ribbons and drawn by six snorting black stallions, and all the cornets and drums of the town band should have broken loose with "Glory O, Glory O, to the Bold Fenian Men."

What funeral could my grandfather have been given except the one he got? The sombre hymns were sung, and he was sent to his Maker by the United Church minister, who spoke, as expected, of the fact that Timothy Connor had been one of Manawaka's pioneers. He had come from Ontario to Manitoba by Red River steamer, and he had walked from Winnipeg to Manawaka, earning his way by shoeing horses. After some years as a blacksmith, he had enough money to go into the hardware business. Then he had built his house. It had been the first brick house in Manawaka. Suddenly the minister's recounting of these familiar facts struck me as though I had never heard any of it before.

I could not cry. I wanted to, but I could not. When it became compulsory to view the body, after the accepted custom, I had to force myself to my feet. I had never looked upon a dead face before.

He looked exactly the same as he had in life. The same handsome eagle-like features. His eyes were closed. It was only when I noticed the closed eyes that I knew that the blue ice of his stare would never blaze again. I was not sorry that he was dead. I was only surprised. Perhaps I had really imagined that he was immortal. Perhaps he even was immortal, in ways which it would take me half a lifetime to comprehend.

Afterwards, we went back to the Brick House. Wes did not drink, but he had provided himself with a mickey of rye.

"C'mon," he said. "This'll do all of you good."

"I'm not saying no," Aunt Edna replied. "How about you, Beth?"

"I guess so," my mother said. "I feel as though I've been put through a wringer."

"You know something, Beth?" Aunt Edna went on. "I can't believe he's dead. It just doesn't seem possible."

"I know what you mean," my mother said. "Edna —were we always unfair to him?"

My aunt swallowed a mouthful of rye and ginger ale.

"Yes, we were," she said. "And he was to us, as well."

I finished my drink and then I went outside. The old stable-garage had not been entered by anyone in a long time. Probably the key to the padlock on the door had been lost years ago. I got in through the loose boards in the loft, as I had done when I was a child. It was not so simple now, for I was neither as skinny nor as agile as I had been when twelve.

The MacLaughlin-Buick had altered. Its dark brown paintwork had lost its lustre. The beige and brown striped plush of the seats had stiffened and faded. Rust grew on it like patches of lichen on a gravestone.

I wondered what the car might have meant to

him, to the boy who walked the hundred miles from Winnipeg to Manawaka with hardly a cent in his pockets. The memory of a memory returned to me now. I remembered myself remembering driving in it with him, in the ancient days when he seemed as large and admirable as God.

Twenty years later, I went back to Manawaka again. I had not been back in all that time, and I sensed that this would be my last sight of it, for there was nothing to take me there any more. Everything had changed in the family which had been my childhood one, but now I had another family and my own elder child was already fourteen. After my grandfather died, my mother had sold the Brick House and moved to Vancouver. My brother had grown up and married and moved once again. Wes Grigg had been transferred to Nova Scotia, and Aunt Edna's letters were full of the old indomitability?

My mother had died. She was buried in the Manawaka cemetery under the black granite stone of the MacLeods, beside Ewen, her husband and my father, who had died so long before her. Of all the deaths in the family, hers remained unhealed in my mind longest.

I drove out to the town one day, when I was visiting in Winnipeg. I went alone. It would have no meaning for anyone else. I was not even sure it would have any meaning for me. But I went. I went to the cemetery and looked at the granite and the names. I realised from the dates on the stone that my father had died when he was the same age as I was now. I remembered saying things to my children that my mother had said to me, the clichés of affection, perhaps inherited from her mother. *It's a poor family can't afford one lady. Many hands make light work. Let not the sun go down upon your wrath.*

I did not go to look at Grandfather Connor's grave. There was no need. It was not his monument.

I parked the car beside the Brick House. The caragana hedge was unruly. No one had trimmed it properly that summer. The house had been lived in by strangers for a long time. I had not thought it would hurt me to see it in other hands, but it did. I wanted to tell them to trim their hedges, to repaint the window-frames, to pay heed to repairs. I had feared and fought the old man, yet he proclaimed himself in my veins. But it was their house now, whoever they were, not ours, not mine.

I looked at it only for a moment, and then I drove away.

ABOUT THE AUTHOR

MARGARET LAURENCE was born in 1926 in Neepawa, a small town in Manitoba. In 1960 her novel *This Side Jordan* was published in the United States, England and Canada and won for her Canada's Beta Sigma Phi Award for the best novel by a Canadian. Following this were *The Prophet's Camel Bell*, a book about Somaliland (published in the U.S. as *New Wind in a Dry Land*); *The Tomorrow-Tamer*, a collection of short stories; and *The Stone Angel*, a novel. In 1967 her novel *A Jest of God* won the Governor General's Award; it later became the basis for the film *Rachel, Rachel*. *The Fire-dwellers* (1969) was followed by a collection of short stories, *A Bird in the House* (1970). Her other works include *Jason's Quest*, a children's story; *Long Drums and Cannons*, a study of Nigerian literature; and *The Diviners*, which won the 1974 Governor General's Award. Her most recent book, *Heart of a Stranger*, a volume of personal essays, was published in 1976. In 1972 Margaret Laurence was made a Companion of the Order of Canada, the highest award given by the Canadian government.

SEAL BOOKS

Offers you a list of outstanding fiction, non-fiction and classics of Canadian literature in paperback by Canadian authors, available at all good bookstores throughout Canada.

The Mark of Canadian Bestsellers

THE MANAWAKA SERIES

by
Margaret Laurence,

Canada's most celebrated novelist,
Winner of the Governor-General's Award

The Manawaka stories, set in the most famous fictional town in Canada, offer a clear-eyed vision of Canadian land and people.

This skilled story teller balances humor and pathos as she portrays the human condition through characters struggling to come to terms with themselves and with the world.

☐ 01720-5	**THE FIRE-DWELLERS**	$2.95
☐ 01740-X	**A JEST OF GOD**	$3.25
☐ 01742-6	**A BIRD IN THE HOUSE**	$2.95
☐ 01778-7	**THE STONE ANGEL**	$3.50
☐ 01787-6	**THE DIVINERS**	$3.95

Seal Books are available in paperback in bookstores across Canada, or use this handy coupon.

McClelland & Stewart-Bantam Ltd., Dept. CS
60 St. Clair Ave. East, Suite 601, Toronto, Ont.,
Canada M4T 1N5

Please send me the book(s) checked above. I am enclosing $_____, including $1.00 to cover postage and handling. Send cheque or money order—no cash or C.O.D.'s please.

Mr/Mrs/Miss_____

Address_____

City_____ Province_____

Country_____ Postal Code_____

Please allow 4 to 6 weeks for delivery. This offer expires 8/83.

MSML-3

Gramley Library
Salem College
Winston-Salem, NC 27108